IN THE BELLY OF THE WHALE

A NOVEL BY DON BAILEY

This book is for real people, especially Anne and Jane.

I hear the strange noises
pain brings
I am separate from
the tolling of the bell
distanced from friend's voices
I detect whispers
but feel the penetration
of my own death
I scream and huddle close
to this sound:

strangers are wounds
I touch
and sometimes heal

I do not understand
the silence
of their wholeness:

once in the belly
of a fish
I felt whole

I understood the walls
that shielded me from the shore:

now there is too much space
I see others
I run toward the sound
and it is gone before I arrive:

in the belly of the fish
I was still
I knew everything
there were no sounds
life and death
were reasonable answers
to no questions:

I was deaf

hearing has brought me fear.

If I were Franz Kafka having a Canadian nightmare I'd have wakened up to find I'd turned into a large beaver. And you could have had me for a nickel. Canadian of course. But instead the ghost of Red Ryan slithered up my pant leg and together with old tunes of glory lisping in the hallowed halls of Canada's money-market history, we set out on a tour. A magical mystery tour. But no Beatles. Just their spirit. We heard them in the landscape. Alarms, they call them. All the banks have them. Red hadn't said a word. And after the first shot he was gone. Left me holding the bag, as it were. Gone. Him and Gabby Hayes and all the Howdy Doody Gang. It was like suddenly growing old. Or having the TV break down in the middle of the late show. And I was alone.

The trouble is I can't forget anything. I haven't robbed a bank in . . . Christ years. Years. From a model prisoner to a model citizen in four short years via intensive rehabilitation and therapy. I'm glad now that all that therapy was at the public's expense. But I'm still not sure why.

Before I didn't even know I had dreams. Now I can never forget them. I'll never forget the first time the psychologist asked me: had any dreams recently? What fuckin' dreams? Sometimes I wake up screaming. You wanna hear about that? I mean, everybody does that. Don't they? But I didn't give him a smart-ass answer. He was a nice man. The chaplain of the prison who was also a psychologist. He'd just got his degree and I was the first up to bat on the new pitch. And his wife made him coffee every morning, which he brought in a thermos and let me drink. It never had sugar in it and he always forgot to bring some. So did I.

I first put a request slip in to see him because of my wife and because of a sermon he gave. I never went to church but I'd heard about the sermon because one of the guys threatened to punch him in the mouth in the middle of it. The guy was thrown in the hole and the sermon continued. It was about love. The reverend was saying that the reason a lot of guys were in prison was because they really didn't know what love was all about. They couldn't give it or take it. That's a little rough when for the past two or three years you've been sitting in your cell saying the only reason you're there is because some bastard squealed on you. So I went to see him out of a kind of curiosity and to see if he could get my wife off my back. She was always writing letters about love and other, less disturbing subjects but still things that bugged me. My kids missed me.

"I've watched you," he said. "I wondered when you'd come."

I was sitting in his office drinking my first cup of thermos coffee and trying to figure out a way to get him to do what I wanted without getting too involved in the thing myself. I was watching him and not listening very well. I liked the way he looked. A man my size, small, five-two or so, but fatter than me. Not really fat, maybe pudgy, so when he smiled his face wrinkled a lot, not like mine, which just gets tight because the skin has to stretch so much. And he had blue eyes like me too, only paler and brighter too in some way that made you think he was always laughing, which in a way I guess he was. People always say my eyes are cold.

He was like a tailor, the way he talked, his fingers always moving like he was stitching each word in the air for you to see. And then he said, "You know, you really are a charming person."

Was the guy a gear box? I mean, there was something sissy about the guy, his hands always moving, the constant smile showing the black part of his teeth that the gold caps didn't cover. And his silver hair, what was left of it, was kind of suspicious the way it stayed in place so perfectly. Maybe the guy was a swish. But he wore crumby clothes. Crumby's not the right word, but what he wore wasn't right for a swish. For instance that day he had a pair of brown pants that were sort of shiny. Probably because they were old. And they had cuffs. And he had a tweed jacket with the tweed fast wearing out, what was left curling up into little balls that hung like burrs.

He was Dutch. Maybe that explains everything.

"I've watched you with the other men," he said. "The way you operate. You must always get what you want, eh?"

And he smiled.

"I've never thought of it like that," I said.

"Oh com'on, Joseph, I think we're going to be friends but we musn't lie to each other. I get a request from you to talk about your wife, so I do a little checking and I find Joseph Cross is being badgered by the correspondence officer to write to his wife, to at least answer some of her letters. Apparently Mrs. Cross has even written the warden. Joseph Cross, it seems plain, doesn't want to write her so he needs someone to run interference. Correct?"

8

He poured me another cup of coffee and waited.

I didn't say anything. Sometimes that's the best way.

"She must love you very much," he said. "How long is it now?"

"Three years since I've seen her."

"And the children?"

"Yeah, same thing."

"So?"

"Yeah, so you're right. I want them off my back. She's even got the kids sending me notes they write themselves. Can hardly read the goddam things, they write so lousy, so what's the point? They think I'm in a hospital, so let me die here. They make me tired. I just want to do my time."

It's funny how mad I was feeling. My voice was loud. Deek was right about the charm thing. I spent a lot of my time smiling even though it hurt my face. I never got angry. Not out loud anyway. So what was happening?

"I don't think we're going to settle this today, Joseph. What I'd like to do is get together with you on a regular basis a couple of times a week and talk it through."

I felt tired. Usually I felt smooth like a glider, no strings attached, floating around, and like there was a secret wind from somewhere that kept me in movement and kept anyone from getting their hands on me.

"All right," I said. "I don't see what good it'll do to talk, but we'll talk."

"Tomorrow," he said. "I'll have the guard pick you up at work. Where are you?"

"In school full time."

"Studying?"

"English."

"Oh. And someday you're going to write a story about all this."

Fuck you, Jack, it's a good stall.

"Sure," I said and gave my most innocent smile. Somehow I knew his was more convincing.

That night I had my first dream. I was on a ship I was directing to some point in the ocean where I knew there was buried treasure. The journey was vague in its details, there was a light but no sun. The sky was grey and there were no clouds except maybe one huge one, but

9

it had no definition. It was a soundless journey with even the ocean lying still like a dead thing and the ship glided through it silently. I had no map but the boat stopped automatically at the spot. I put on diving gear and entered the water. In a few moments I found the chest. It had been easy, the water was clear and still but I had trouble getting the chest on board. I hadn't brought anyone to help me. I found a rope and dived again. When the rope was tied securely to the chest I surfaced again, got on the boat and hauled the thing up.

It wasn't locked and when I opened it as I suspected I found it empty, but there was a note, quite dry and folded twice. I opened it and read: YOU SHOULD NOT HAVE COME HERE. 7 October, 1942. My birthday.

I don't remember the trip back. Maybe there wasn't one. But the part I remembered was so clear in my mind that when I woke up I got up right away and flushed my razor blades down the toilet.

The next day with Deek he asked me about dreams and I looked at all the books on the shelves around the room and began to make one up out of book titles. It was fun and it let me think right back to the start when this whole thing started and I was alone.

Except of course the cops kept me company. They had friendship rings for my wrists, the better to show their love, I suppose. And down at the station I kept mum about Red, believing it was better to let sleeping dogs lie. And they didn't press me for much except my finger prints. And we watched the clock together, waiting for me to bring up the topics of discussion, but like always there was nothing to say. The generation gap. But they seemed to understand. They took me to a safe place.

It was there I began to hum. "Take a sad song and make it better," Paul said. What a funny guy. But a sensitive soul, don't you think? And the Don Jail is full of sensitive people. You can't even whistle there. So I hummed. And I liked the porridge in the morning. And the screw who kept everybody locked out and told me about his mortgage and his rotten son with long hair who didn't respect him. And I thought, what a sad song.

But nothing lasts and I met a judge. We did a duo together. I did the Dylan part in the Skyline album, but at the critical moment he shifted into Judas Priest and Frankie Lee, spouting out the finish. The moral of this story, the moral of this song. . . . Well, you know.

I mean, it was a prison time. A time to love. A time to hate. All that. And every story had a happy ending. But I was laughing because everything was just beginning.

Every good comedy has a chase sequence and one morning a Cadillac started mine. Me and several other refugees. They hustled us with clanking umbilical cords into GM's finest and roared down Yonge Street. But the Keystone Cops weren't waiting at Union Station. Just the train, which I found funny. And during the choo-choo ride, everyone flirted with the dwindling world with rattling feet. People smiled or looked grim and nudged junior, who was busy looking up a mini-skirt. It was a nice way to leave them. I hate silent waving.

Another Caddy at the Kingston station. Luxury and attention were what counted now. And yes, counting too. Careful not to lose us. Like we were birth-stones or something. Their favourites. And it might have been our birthdays because the gate opened and we were born again. The only thing I don't like is blowing out candles. Everyone stops singing and it gets cold in the dark.

Someone once told me Treblinka wasn't so bad. He wasn't a Jew. And I read a book and found out how the front part of the place was built with a false section that made it look like a happy little railway station. And all the people arriving were relieved and happy to have their dreams come true. But they were phony. The dreams, the people dreaming and the station; and it made dying sad. And living too, I guess. Our new world wasn't like that though. Even a guy like Trudeau didn't count.

TV Guide was the bible and every second night half of us got religious. You took your turn at everything. And a young boy who resembled Elizabeth Taylor more and more each day was queen of the TV room. So like most people I wrote Mother, wife and kids and told them I'd signed the pledge and in a year or so I'd drop them another line. Maybe around Christmas. They weren't to worry. I hated the place. Learned my lesson and all. And with a lot of kisses I lied to the old dame, the love of my life, and my darling little off-spring. Like everybody does. Giggling up our sleeves and trying to complain about the birds waking us up in the morning. But really we loved them and if they'd left we'd never have slept. They chose to sing their songs inside. Like us. We understood that. Everybody needs to feel real. Even birds, I guess.

Like one guy who had stolen a truck of wieners. They called him Wiener. A nice touch. Do people like Diefenbaker ever get to feel that real, with other people writing their acts? It's hard to find a little pond to be a big frog in. Maybe that's everybody's problem. No ponds anymore. Or not enough. But we weren't like that. Never worried about being lost. Your neighbour carried you in his eyes and you had only to frisk his face.

Last week I came home to TO. A sensible person now. Everybody tells me that. We all have to believe something. But I was sitting in a bar the other night looking for something familiar when old Red sidled up to me and said, "I meant to write, kid, but I couldn't remember your name."

He was right to forget. memories leave scar-tissue and after a while you can't feel anything. A prison guard told me that once after he locked me in for the night, and you know, if it wasn't for Red, I think I might be missing that guy. Or someone. Even myself.

My father was a thin man. Like a worn dime I once carried for good luck and then forgot and finally lost, I have neglected the memory of him. Like a fish not caught.

He was a tall stringy man whom I remember at the breakfast table drinking a glass of hot water, every morning blowing on his dirty fingers; the printer's ink never really washed out though my mother kept a can of Snap in the bathroom just for him. He ate his porridge and I would stare and stir my cornflakes until they were mush. Friday morning he had bran flakes.

Then he would go to the basement. He operated a small printing business from there. Wedding invitations and business cards were his main line when he first started but every so often he'd get a big job like printing up 10,000 advertising flyers for a 1¢ sale at the local drug-store and my mother and I would help by folding the sheets as they dried.

I had a paper route in those days. I was about eight. And whenever I helped like that in the basement he'd joke and say, "Why don't I take the wages you earned today off the ten bucks you owe me."

"Sure," I'd say. "You betcha."

You betcha was one of his favourite expressions. But it bothered me when he said that about taking my wages off the loan he'd given me to buy the paper route. I'd never saved enough to pay it back and whenever I got close to having it I forgot about it and bought something stupid like the baseball glove that I couldn't use because I had a bad heart and wasn't allowed to play sports.

So the sometimes that I helped him and he said that I felt bad. Like I was always paying back and I couldn't do him a favour or something.

When I was nine I got so sick that I had to sell my paper route back to the same guy I'd bought it from and he'd only pay seven dollars. He claimed I'd lost too many of his customers, which was true I suppose. I used to daydream a lot and miss customers and instead leave the paper at some stranger's. Anyway I had to sell it so I took the seven but when I offered it to the old man, he pulled his mouth tight, shook his head and said, "Nope, you save 'er. You'll need 'er for Christmas presents."

I put the money in my bottom drawer with my socks and somehow managed not to spend it. For Christmas I bought my mother a bottle of sickly smelling cologne that was in a bottle shaped like a candle. Aunt Ruth, who was really my mother's mother, which made her my grandmother but she didn't like that title, received a sewing kit with twelve spools of different-coloured thread. I bought Boots, my dog, one of those chocolate-flavoured rubber bones. But no matter how hard I try I can't remember what I got my father. Probably a flat-50 of Export cigarettes, plain. But I'm not sure. I always bought him a flat-50. Somehow I'd like to think I bought him something different.

My first memories have to do with noise. The sound of the old letter-press pumping in the basement. The card is placed in the holder by my father and, like a yawning mouth, the machine opens and closes in a constant cycle, nimble fingers placing the card, mouth closing card printed, pulled out and another one inserted. Sometimes he worked all night on rush jobs and the only thing louder in the whole world than the noise downstairs was my own pulse and heavy breathing.

The very first sound I remember was screaming. My own. I was on a swing and an old woman in black was pushing me higher and higher. And I screamed louder and louder. It gave me nightmares remembering and my mother explained. That's all it was, a nightmare.

I guess I was about ten when one night I woke up to another sound. It came from my parents' bedroom. My head was pressed up against the wall because I liked the cool feel of it and somehow that noise from the next room came to me. It was my father. He was grunting. And I heard wet sounds that I knew were my mother's kisses. He was saying things but I couldn't make out the words, she just kept agreeing: huh, huh, huh. It was like the letter-press but more scary. When my father worked it was the machine that made the noise. He never once even whistled. Now there was a sound coming from the room where he slept and he was part of it, grunting. I put my hand on the hard thing between my legs and pumped it up and down, put a card in, take it out, until I fell asleep.

I guess after that night my father was more human to me, which was too bad because I wasn't ready for it. But maybe I never would have been. Part of the problem was I didn't understand about sex yet. I still didn't have the nerve to say cunt out loud in the schoolyard like some of the other guys my age did. But the word cooze, when I said it to myself, made my thing hard. So what I understood about sex that made my father more human was that it was something that a man and a woman did together; that there had to be some co-operation involved. I had never seen my mother and father do anything together. He played golf on the weekends and when we went up to the cottage he was always away golfing. He never let me caddy for him, but sometimes he'd let me come and watch and one day a man in the clubhouse tried to talk him into turning pro. The old man just laughed. More like a snort. He didn't laugh out loud like most people. It seemed to get caught in his throat and go back down and all you got was some kind of snort or sneeze. And my mother who did laugh out loud, too loud most of the time, she had her bingo. Mondays and Wednesdays in the city and every night except Sunday at the cottage. Even when we drove up to the cottage we didn't do it together. Not really. I had a kaleidoscope I used to put up to my eyes and turn and turn, and small jig-saw puzzles to play with, and my mother sat in the front and read one of those nurse novels that have a picture of a handsome doctor on the front cover with a blonde and brunette nurse sort of lurking in the background. My poor mother was always having her hair dyed blonde or brunette, every month she switched from one to the other. Sometimes twice in one month. She was never satisfied that it was the right shade.

"Wilf," she'd say, looking up from the book. "What in hell's name are ya doin'?"

"Just turned off the key," he'd say.

"My God, we're going 70 miles an hour. You wanna kill us, doin' someting like that?"

"We're on a hill, Marg. Going down. It saves gas."

"Gonna kill us onea these days," she'd say.

I liked it when he did things like that but it wasn't something that made us close so I guess him having sex with her made him human because it was something, to my understanding anyway, that made you that way with another person. But it didn't feel quite natural.

The next summer when I was ten I got sent away to my grandparents' cottage. My father's parents. Something was wrong at home. All spring my mother had cried a lot. She cried at the slightest thing. I got a D in spelling and she cried. Usually she smacked me.

The day after school closed for the summer my father drove me up to his parents' cottage just outside of Orillia. I wasn't even sure where I was going.

"We won't be openin' our place this year," he said about 50 miles out. "You'll be stayin' with grandma for the summer. Oke doky?"

"You betcha," I said, but I was a bit scared. His parents were really old and they always worried about me and that made me nervous. And I wanted to ask him about my dog, Boots, but I knew they didn't like animals unless they were big fat cats so I didn't say anything.

He never turned the key off when we went down long hills and I thought if he only did it once I'd tell him how much I liked it when he did that. But he didn't.

We stopped at a Sunoco station where he had a credit card and he bought me a hamburger, which my mother would never do because she said the grease was bad for my skin.

"When you come back home, you'll have a brother or sister," he said.

We were on the dirt road very close to the cottage when he said that. I hardly had time to think about it and I didn't know what I should say, and he was opening the door and

16

my grandmother was smothering me, which she always did in front of other people.

"Give me his bag, Wilf, and I'll take it upstairs," my grandfather said.

"You bring yer fishing rod, Joseph?" he asked me.

"Yes sir."

"Yer stayin' fer lunch, Wilf?" my grandmother said.

"Gotta get back. She's really bad. Hated to even leave her today. The doctor says she might have to go in a month early."

And then he turned to me, my father; he seemed to be a very tall man, later I learned he was just average in height, but a thin man, he was always a thin man with short rusty-coloured hair that was turning grey. He had dull brown eyes that did nothing to light up the pale freckly skin of his face that was wrinkled like a potato except for the cheeks that formed strangely smooth pouches as if he kept something in his mouth all the time. To me his cheeks were the thing that made him secretive, everything else was so plain, explainable. I knew the wine-coloured cardigan he wore so well. He wore it in the shop downstairs and when he went golfing. The brown baggy pants were his going-out pants, he wore them golfing or whenever he went out for business. He had a grey pair he wore in the shop, but they had printer's ink from where he wiped his hands all day. And flannel shirts. I don't know how many he had, they all looked alike, but spring, summer, fall and winter he wore one. And every year at Christmas, wearing a flannel shirt, wine-coloured cardigan and brown baggy pants he'd play Santa Claus and hand out the presents from under the tree to Mom and me and in one of the boxes for him there'd always be a new flannel shirt from someone. And he'd smile and his little round cheeks would rise up so high they'd almost block out his eyes. . . . It's kind of funny when you think about it because the last time I talked to my mother she said he was going into the hospital for a cataract operation.

But that was the way I measured my father's mood; the

17

level of his cheeks. That day they hung low, as if they were deflated.

"You behave yourself, Joseph. Mind what you're told and write your mother once a week."

And then he did the strangest thing. He bent over and kissed me. I couldn't remember him ever doing that before and the only time he ever touched me after that was once when he hit me.

He had no teeth and my mother was always nagging him to put in the false ones he had that cost over $200 but he never did, so his mouth was sunken in with the lips set back so really only his chin with its bristles rubbed against my mouth but it really scared me. I remember thinking, I never want to see this man cry.

The summer I was ten probably was the most important period in my family's life. My father moved the business from the basement to a small building a mile from home that used to be a storage garage for trucks. My father and his father ripped out the huge garage doors and built a 40-foot extension on the place. They found a bank that was being demolished and bought the front doors from it and when they were hung in place with their brass knobs shiny, the plant was official. A dream. And my father had a big sign made and placed down near the road away from the parking area: FAIR PRESS.

The doors had to come off again later in the summer when a new automatic press arrived all the way from Germany, and was too big to get inside with the doors on. And my father hired two men to help him and before the summer was over, another one to do deliveries.

Our backyard was dug up and cement steps replaced the wooden ones leading to the basement door. And the basement where my father had his workshop was made into a recreation room by covering the walls with insulation and putting wood panelling over that.

I wasn't there then but my grandfather drove back to the cottage on the weekends and over supper of dumplings and roast beef he'd tell my grandmother the news. I just had to listen.

"The crazy bugger is workin' himself inta the ground," my grandfather would say.

"Listen to the pot callin' the kettle black," she'd say. "Yer just as bad. At yer age tryin' to do a boy's work. It's okay fer him, with a baby comin' and about time at his age, he wants to have things set. But there's no excuse fer you."

"It's my grandchild," grandpa would say, but he never won an argument with her; not that it mattered, he always did what he wanted anyway.

I wrote my mother every week like my father had said and once she sent me a postcard that said now I had my own room in the basement to set up my electric train in and I wouldn't have to take it down like I used to.

In August my mother gave birth to a son. My grandmother told me.

"Well, they got her in the hospital. Cut her open to get it. Wonder it didn't kill her but boys are always big. Over twelve pounds. May kill her yet. They got her in one of those tents with oxygen. Both should've known better. Too old to be havin' kids."

We were alone when she told me. She was making supper on the wood stove. Roast beef and dumplings. Every night the same. Not night really. We ate at three in the afternoon and around seven there was salad and sandwiches if you wanted them.

I never liked my grandmother much. She was too old to have any patience left for anything but the aches in her own bones. She plodded irritably through a daily routine that was probably taught to her by her mother and if interfered with by anything like bad news, only answered, I told you so.

But I got the feeling she was proud of my brother's birth. She let it interfere. When the telephone rang and she received the news she sat there looking kind of stunned, I mean she forgot to keep pushing her glasses up over her nose for a few minutes and even her voice seemed higher-pitched when she told me, less growly. And then instead of asking me for the tenth time that day whether or not I'd had a bowel movement, she went back to the phone and called other relatives who'd probably already heard. And the calls of course were long distance.

I didn't think much about my brother. That part didn't seem real but my mother. . . . Almost died. Wonder it didn't kill her. May kill her yet. All those thoughts bunched in my brain like a berserk ping-pong ball.

Then I'd be an orphan. And I discovered I enjoyed being sad. The rest of the afternoon I forgot to kill frogs down at the river's edge. I didn't play on the swing my grandfather had put up especially for me. I walked through the rasberry bushes cutting my arms and hands until they bled and I was gloriously sad because I was alone with no mother. An orphan.

My grandmother had angina and beside her bed she kept a bottle of little white pills for the pain. That night for some reason I went up to bed when she told me, walked into her room, took about six of the pills and swallowed them. I lay in my own bed feeling delighted with myself but scared too.

When I woke up vomiting I wondered seriously for the first time what it would be like to die. Everybody would be sorry. But for what? I wasn't sure. And then my grandmother came in. She brought a pan for me to be sick in.

"How many times have I told ya to wear a hat," she said. "Fer sure you've got sunstroke. God, I told ya so many times."

And I kind of laughed inside because if I was to die, Grandma would feel sorry that she hadn't got me to wear a hat. She'd blame herself for me getting sunstroke and dying. It really felt good, thinking that.

In the morning I felt weak and a bit dizzy. She wanted me to stay in bed but didn't insist when I said I felt okay and I was going to pick some raspberries for our lunch and if I felt sick at all or too hot I'd come inside. I think she was always glad when I was out of sight, she could worry a little less about me. And there were still phone calls to make about the birth as I discovered when I listened at the door after I was supposed to have left.

"Operator, I wanna call Toronto, person to person with Wilfred Fair. . . ."

She was calling my father for more details. I was safe.

I walked down to the edge of the property, beautiful green sloping lawn that stretched for 75 yards from the back porch with a babington net strung between two young trees; I stood at the edge and looked back at the white building, like a castle to me with nine bedrooms. I saw the bird-bath my grandfather had made from cement and field-stone was starting to sink into the ground on an angle, and one of the red-and-white wooden lawn-chairs was turned on its side. I walked over to the swing that hung between two huge elm trees and kicked at it. It came back and hit me in the knee. And I remember laughing at that. And then I grabbed the seat and sat down and swung back and forth until I started to cry. I couldn't stop the word coming to my mind: brother. And I couldn't stop the picture in my mind of standing in the garage behind my home in Toronto with my arm around a boy and his around me and we were both saying: someday we'll both run away . . . and then the words got faint and I didn't know what else we said or even why we said what we did. But HE was my brother.

Everything seemed to have changed, but I knew really nothing had. So I cried because I didn't feel like killing frogs and because it seemed the best way to feel sorry for myself was to feel sorry I'd ever killed them in the first place. And I tried to tell myself a story about the frogs I'd killed who were gone to heaven except the beautiful meadow I imagined as frog heaven had another boy in it who was killing them all over again and he was the boy in the garage. My brother.

So then I decided. I got up, walked to the edge of the dock, continued out fifteen to its end and stared down into the clear blue water of the Severn River. I could see the small perch and sunfish chasing the schools of minnows my grandfather and I sometimes dipped for with his big net when we needed bait. I watched them play for a long time and began to forget everything when I gave them names and tried to keep track of them. But it got too hard. My head hurt from the strain and I stood up and fell in the water, probably on purpose.

It may have been that I heard the car pull in the driveway. I don't remember but I suppose I did. I was only in the water for a few seconds and I heard feet pounding along the wharf. It sounded funny from under the water, like an echo. My eyes were open and I was looking up and suddenly a face was looking down at me. I wanted to laugh, it was like one of those crazy mirrors at the exhibition that make you look all crooked. And then the face moved and something terrible swooshed through the water to destroy the mirror and grabbed at my neck. I thought of a shark and opened my mouth to scream and swallowed a lot of water while the thing dragged me to the surface.

I passed out. Later I found out it was my cousin Bob. He was about nineteen then and he'd driven up with his father, my father's brother, to tell Grandma more details of my mother's condition. He'd seen me from the car as I was going in, ran down and hauled me up with Grandpa's fish gaff. He even gave me artificial respiration. When I woke up in bed later I was glad it was him. His father was always calling him dirty names and now he was a hero.

My father arrived the next morning.

"I don't know what's got into him the last couplea days, Wilf," my grandmother said. "He's been doin' the craziest things. Not wearin' a hat, gettin' sunstroke. Got cuts all over him from God knows where. And then fallin' in the river. It's a miracle Bob was there just at the right time."

"I'll take him off your hands a few days," he said.

"So, what's been goin' on?" he asked that day when we were driving back.

"I hate wearin' that stupid hat Grandpa gave me. It's too big an' it keeps falling off and then I get sick. An' then I get dizzy and I don't know what I'm doing and I fall off the dock."

22

It felt kind of bad saying that and not saying what had really happened but I still wasn't sure what had. And I got the feeling that a lot of the time when I spoke to him I was always making up excuses for something I'd done or didn't do.

"Well," he said. "How'd ya like to help me for a few days and then you can earn enough to buy yourself a new hat. Your own hat."

"You betcha," I said. And I was really happy and slept in the car when it got dark and had good dreams.

I woke up and my father was carrying me into the house. I pretended I was asleep and he slung me over his shoulder when we reached the front door and he unlocked it. It was quiet and dark without my mother there, like he was dead, and he took me all the way up to my room hung over his shoulder, stopping to flick on lights, and he never bumped me into anything once. I thought I must be smiling when he undressed me but he didn't say anything so it must have been just inside. I could smell him, sort of like rusty iron mixed with cigarette smoke.

In the morning we both ate cornflakes.

"There's three other boys we're going to meet for the job today," he said.

"Okay," I said.

"D'ya know what we're doin'?"

"No."

"I've got about ten, twelve thousand flyers gotta be put out for the field-day before tomorrow night. Think we can do it?"

"You betcha," I said.

"Well, if you get tired you stop, right?"

"Sure, but I won't."

"But if you do, right?"

"Yeah."

The way he said that, like he expected me to keel over at the second door. He never said that but something in his voice and his eyes, they were both flat but it always felt like a sneer.

I'd show him.

We worked in pairs. One guy on one side of the street and one on the other. We each had a canvas bag that held about 200 of the flyers. From the moment he let me and my partner out of the car I began ro run. Going across lawns, jumping small fences, crashing through hedges, but making sure each flyer was either inside the door or milk-box, not like my partner who just threw them on the porch. By the time I was finished my side the other guy still had more than a third to go so I crossed and raced along to meet him.

"What's the big hurry?" he said.

"It's fun."

"Shit, at 30¢ an hour, no use killin' yourself."

He was older than me by a year or two and I'd never met him before. I always wanted older boys to like me, maybe because I was so small, but I also wanted to show the old man.

"Well, I'll probably get slower when it gets hotter," I said.

"I don't care, but the old bugger sees you workin' yer ass off and he'll still crack the whip at ya."

He talked like he didn't know who I was. It excited me for some reason.

"You worked for him before?" I said.

"Yeah, a couple a times. Tight as a Jew. This yer first time?"

"Yeah."

"Well, just watch him, he'll try an' get as much from ya as he can and he won't pay no extra. Here he comes now."

My father drove us to the next street without saying anything. He dropped us at a corner and said, "There you go. See you in half an hour."

"See what I mean," my partner said. "Half an hour! Christ it'll take us at least an hour. Look at all them hills we gotta go up and down."

But I began running again. Tripping over wires that were strung across lawns that were meant to prevent the likes of me from tromping across them. I raced from one house to the next, sweating, folding and plotting shortcuts, with one eye on the road watching for my father's green Chev so he'd see me in action. But it was hard to keep my mind on anything else but the weight slung around my neck. Already it was beginning to dig in and rub raw where I was sweating. I got to playing a game with myself where I wouldn't allow myself to think about the weight until I'd done ten houses and then I'd comment to myself that see, the bag was much, much lighter. And again I finished my side of the street way before my partner.

"Ain't you hot?" he said when we met again.

"Dyin'," I said.

"Ya think that cheap old prick'd buy us a pop? No way."

"Maybe we could ask somebody at one of the houses for a glass a water," I said.

"You go ahead. They won't."

I felt brave and strong with the bag off my neck and sitting beside the curb, finished my job for the moment and waiting for my father. I walked up to the first house and knocked. A woman with hair curlers like my mother and pedal pushers answered.

"Uh huh."

"My friend and me were wondering if we could have a glass a water," I said.

I was nervous with my stomach pulled in tight. She had the look my mother calls saucy, head slanted, eyes bright and sort of smiling like she already knows what you're going to say and is waiting for you to get it over with, not in a bad way, kind of pleasant but my mother calls it saucy.

"We've been delivering the handbills about the field-day," I said. "An' it's kinda hot."

"You're not kiddin'," she said.

I really liked the way she said that. Like I could kid her if I wanted to.

"Tell your friend to com'on over an' you can come in and have some lemonade. I already made some for myself."

"Hey com'on," I called. I didn't know his name. He didn't know mine either.

We each had two glasses and we both said very little, though the woman talked a lot, not to anybody in particular, and I liked to hear her voice and sometimes she'd try to catch you and she'd say, "An' whattya think of that?"

I liked that game so I'd listen real careful and pretty near always have something to say. The other guy always got caught and toward the end most of her talking was in my direction.

"I guess we gotta go," he said finally. "Thanks a lot."

"Oke doky. Anytime kids."

"Thank you," I said.

But outside my new friend became quite animated as we stood on the curb waiting for the car.

"Christ, that was really good. Didja see the boobs on 'er? With all those buttons undone I could see right down. Boy, she really likes gettin' it."

He made me nervous talking that way. I had noticed the cleavage down the front of her blouse but I didn't think of her like that. I mean I'd seen mother's a couple of times when I was younger. They just hung there the way I remember them and jiggled when she walked around. They weren't remarkable or anything like the pictures I'd seen that older guys cut out of magazines and brought to school. Those gave you a hard-on. But I didn't feel like that about the woman who gave us lemonade even if she did have some buttons undone. If I were really an orphan she was the kind of person I could just walk up to the door and tell her all about it and she'd tilt her head sideways, look inside me with those bright eyes, give a pleasant laugh and everything would be okay. And if a person ever felt like crying it'd be okay to put your head hard against her soft chest, even if the buttons were undone.

My father showed up a few minutes later and the same procedure was repeated.

"Pick you up in half an hour," he said. "Youse got enough. Maybe you better take a few more."

I did but my partner stalled and asked, "When's lunch?"

"Oh it's early," my father said. "Got plenty a time to do at least a couple more."

So the marathon began again. This time though I ran to forget. At the first mail-box the bag was chewing into the bone in my shoulder, my intake of breath was like a razor slash across my throat, my trembling legs when I looked down at them were thin like my mother had always said and they were cut and itched from the bushes I'd scrambled through. I began to feel sorry for myself. A pleasant game and I kept thinking of returning to the woman in curlers and pedal-pushers that night all cut and bleeding, my tongue hanging down past my short pants, and falling unconscious at her feet. And I felt myself being lifted and carried safely to a soft bed. And then hands touched me and took off my clothes and covered me. And I fell asleep smiling inside.

It was like a serial film in my mind. I couldn't get past the first reel and it was projected over and over again in my mind until by the end of the street it was sort of blurry and scratched. But it kept my mind occupied.

At last it was time for lunch. My father had the other boys in the car when he picked up my partner and me. He drove to a nearby park and let them out. I wasn't sure what to do. They'd all brought lunches in paper bags and I hadn't thought of doing that. I got out of the car when everybody else did and waited.

"I'll be back for you in an hour," he said, and they dispersed, scrambling away like frightened gnats. I almost ran off with them when my father called, "Com'on Joseph, hop in."

"I thought maybe I should've brought a lunch," I said after he pulled away.

"How ya feelin'?"

"Great," I lied.

"I seen ya," he said. "Built like that ya move like a rabbit. That other character's like an elephant. Slower than molasses."

That's all he said but it made me forget everything, the

pain, the tiredness, even the woman in pedal-pushers and curlers.

Instead of driving home like I expected, he stopped at a restaurant. It was a small place, kind of dark and not very fancy but it smelled good. And when we walked in, a woman yelled out, "Hey, here's Wolf!" It sounded sort of like *woolf*, the way she said it, as if she couldn't pronounce his name right.

"Hiya, Wolf," she said and put her arms around him.

"Hey, this must be the kid, eh?"

"Yeah, this is Joseph."

"Hi," she said and stuck out her hand. "I'm Bernice. I knew ole Wolfy here before anybody. We used to go to school together."

She didn't look as old as my father. But when I looked up at him, his cheeks were pushed up tight, squeezing out his eyes, and his mouth was stretched tight with the lips curled inward; the way he smiles. He looked like he could be younger.

We sat at a booth and she hovered and flapped around like a bird. She looked older than my mother in one way but younger in another. She was wearing a white waitress uniform that was all lumpy so she'd lost her figure, which my mother hadn't completely done even though she was a bit fat, and the woman's face was smooth except for some creases around her mouth and eyes that showed a lot when she laughed, which was okay because they looked nice, dimples my mother called them, my mother didn't have them, she wore make-up so you couldn't see any lines or marks in her face. The woman's hair was black but there were some parts of it that were turning grey, which looked funny mostly because it was in pig-tails. She was hard to figure out but I thought I liked her, the way she kept shifting around on her feet like she couldn't hold still and the way she talked, like she had a million secrets to tell you, just you sort of. But in another way she was like the girls at school, giggling a lot and talking about stuff that I couldn't figure out.

"What's good?" my father asked.

"Pork hocks," she said. "You want some? I had 'em on since early this morning. An' cabbage."

He looked at me. God I didn't even know what they were. Pork hocks? A lot of times my mother gave me hot dogs or hamburgers at lunch and sometimes Kraft dinner but never pork hocks. And we never had them for supper. Only sometimes we had a pork roast.

"Give us two," he said.

"An' how about some buttermilk?" she said. "Got some good an' cold."

He looked at me again.

"It's good on hot days," he said.

"Sure," I said, though I'd never heard of the stuff.

"Two, Berny."

She called the order through a slot and came back.

"So how about the new one?" She said. "How're they both doin'?"

"Good," he said. "She's comin' outa the oxygen soon, this week probably, and the boy's good. I could take him home but then I'd have to get somebody to look after him."

"I would!" she said.

"He's just as well there."

"Whataya callin' him?" she said.

"Daniel," he said. "Daniel Francis."

"A Danny boy," she said and clapped her hands. "Has he got red hair?"

"Nope, blond. But there's plenty of it."

"Isn't that lovely. God, you must really be happy, Wolf."

He didn't say anything, just smoked his cigarette and looked off somewhere.

"Hey, dinner's here," she said.

She left us alone while we ate. Everything was boiled; usually my mother fried or roasted our meat for supper but this was delicious. The pork hock was huge but a lot of it was bone and a layer of fat on the outside had to be removed before you could get at the real meat, but once you got to it, it was more tender than roast pork and tasted better. I ate

29

everything, put salt in my buttermilk like my father did and enjoyed the slightly sour taste of the stuff.

"Makes the glass look funny, eh?" he said.

"Yeah," but I was thinking about my brother. Now he had a name. This was the first time I'd heard it. And soon he and my mother would be coming home. I couldn't stop the feeling of disappointment.

Always there had been this dream of an older brother. When I broke something like my electric train I didn't have to hide it away and say I was tired of it, he'd know how to fix it. And he'd teach me how to swim. And we'd box together, he'd teach me and wouldn't smash me hard when I was first learning. He would be like Buck Rogers but there'd be secret passwords between us that only we knew. And he would like me and want to carry me on his shoulders when we took the short-cut across the field at the cottage to go fishing. And if my dog Boots got hit by a car like Tiny had, my brother wouldn't stand there crying like I had, he'd know how to fix her. People would respect him and know that he was my brother. He'd tell them so they'd know. He wouldn't forget me.

It was only an idea, the older brother. I mean he was never really anybody but now with the name Daniel it was hard to keep the idea even.

My father paid for the meal and we went back to work. I remember Bernice kept patting my head while she put her other hand on my father's shoulder.

"See you soon," she said.

He waved and I got in the car without looking back.

Later in the afternoon I was sick. I couldn't know why but I was sure it was going to happen. I got slower and slower and the bag got heavier and heavier and finally I threw up on someone's lawn and my partner came from across the street to help me.

"Geez, I tole ya," he said.

I almost laughed, it was like my grandmother and my head was dizzy and I couldn't walk my legs were so wobbly and suddenly it seemed funny and I laughed. And I kept laughing until he got scared or something and ran off down the street to find my father. I tried to get up but couldn't stop the thing in my throat, it choked me to stop laughing and all the crazy things that went through my head; my partner would be swearing at my old man, calling him a prick for making me work so hard that I got sick and if the woman with the curlers and pedal-pushers from this morning could see me now, she'd be so sorry and say, "You poor little slob, com'on in fer lemonade. What's the bastard tryin' to do, kill ya?" And it was all my fault.

He drove me home in silence.

"Too much to eat," I tried to kid. "I shoulda worn Grandpa's hat. But I'll be okay tomorrow."

I guess I had a fever. He gave me some aspirins and some of the medicine Dr. Waltzinberg from the hospital gave my mother for when I felt weak. I slept all the rest of the afternoon, all night and when I woke up in the morning he was gone. My legs shook when I got up so I stayed in bed most of the day except for the times I spent going through the drawers in their bedroom. That wasn't much fun anymore though because I knew all the stuff that was there and they never seemed to get anything new. My mother's jewelry-case was the most interesting thing with all its old brooches that had funny stones in them and I would make up stories about the stones that were missing, how it was used to ransom one of my cousins who was kinapped when he fell asleep at a matinée on Saturday afternoon when he should have been cutting the lawn anyway. After a while this bored me too and I went back to bed.

He came early.

"How ya feelin'?" he said.

"Fine. Good," I said. "I'm sorry about . . . well, gettin' sick like that."

"You ready to go back to the cottage?" he said.

"Sure. You betcha."

But I wasn't. I was disappointed again. It felt like I'd never have the chance to make up for it. To make things okay. I mean he'd treated me good, special. Taking me to the restaurant, but it'd got spoiled. But then suddenly it didn't seem to matter. I wanted to go back to the cottage. At least there I got left alone in a way. And I knew all of a sudden things were going to be different from now on. I had no idea why but I knew they would be. Part of it was to do with Daniel, I was sure of that but there was something else. Like we had all decided something, even my mother who wasn't there, and none of us had talked about it but it was decided. And I felt good driving back to the cottage with my father even though he didn't say one word to me, that fit in with the new feeling I had too. I knew in a strange way I didn't belong to him anymore or to any of them. It had to do with all the people who didn't know me, like my partner delivering the flyers, the woman in the curlers and the pedal-pushers, the waitress, Bernice and the boy in my dream in the garage who was my real brother, and my pretend older brother and now Daniel; I wasn't like any of them, I was different. And somehow that made me feel safe. And I knew some day it'd make me feel scared but that was okay too.

"School starts in a couple of weeks," my father said when we got there. "I'll be back up then to get you. Your mother'll be home by then too."

"Okay," I said.

"Watch yourself," he said.

What a funny thing to say, I thought. Standing in front of a mirror all day. Or careful to stay in the sun so you don't lose your shadow. Standing at the edge of the dock looking down at your reflection in the water. Watch yourself. Okay I will, if everybody else'll leave me alone and stop watching me. I will.

"I will," I said.

"Here's a couple of bucks, get yourself a hat."

"Thanks a lot."

We stood there quiet, just the two of us. My grandmother had taken my bag inside and my grandfather was sleeping. It was dark and the dew was already in the air. I could hear the crickets and the warble of a night bird. He pulled the zipper on the wine cardigan higher.

"Cold, eh?"

"Yeah," I said, and I realized for the first time in my life that my father was an awkward man. I felt sadness and excitement and wished with all my heart he would tell me something. Just something.

"Guess I better get goin'. Road get's bad Sunday nights. All the traffic going back. So watch yourself, eh?"

"Okay, an' thanks a lot, Dad. Thanks."

He drove away and I stood there a long time trying to figure out why I felt so bad and trying not to feel that way. And wondering why now all of a sudden I felt lonely.

It took me weeks to tell Deek all this. Maybe months. More like months. Drinking sugarless coffee in his office and looking at book titles and just talking. Remembering just this one small part of it and waiting all the time for him to tell me something, give me an explanation, but always him asking me, "Well Joseph, what do you think it means? Don't ask me, Joseph, how do you feel about it?"

I told Deek all this and he didn't tell me anything. But then I remember, neither did my father.

This morning I have the booze shakes. I'm lying on the balcony sweating. It's still very early because the balcony is in the shade. But my mind is racing, burning like I'd been standing in the hot Manitoba sun for an hour. But I'm home, in Toronto. I've been home for three days now. This is the fourth day. (And on the fourth day he created . . . ?) Shit, I never can remember that stuff when it's important. That's the kind of thing that made life worthwhile in prison, when in the morning a thought would come to me in the form of a question and I'd wait all day to see Deek, to ask him, but still trying to figure it out myself. Things to think about like, is it really true that a man has an orgasm when he's hanged? Or remembering something a girl once said about little dots being painted in the digit slots of telephones in order that a person can focus his eye correctly and not dial the wrong number. And Deek pointing out to me that the blue scar that starts at a point almost exactly between my eyes and runs along my left eyebrow was a good thing and I shouldn't get plastic surgery to remove it; people's eyes were drawn to it and they couldn't help looking in my eyes. He said I had nice eyes. He had a way of making you feel good.

Four days ago, just about this time Deek walked me down to the front gate where the station-waggon was waiting to take me to the bus. I'd signed all the papers the day before for my parole and got the gym instructor, the librarian and kitchen people to sign my paper saying I didn't have their knives or forks or gym shoes or books and officially I was released when I got their signatures, especially after the warden gave me his little talk. (Well Joe, you've certainly been a model inmate while you were here. Just goes to show you, you can do it if you want.) I think the words were interchangeable, it sounded like a speech that came in a cardboard box from Ottawa and was printed on plastic blocks. When he signed then it was really official, I was going home. And Deek walked to the gate and shook my hand. It was strange, him shaking my hand. I'd looked at him across the desk for months but I'd never touched him and it was a surprise to feel how tough his hands were,

34

thick skin like a labourer but soft in their touch, gentle. And it made me remember that he once said he liked gardening.

I'm lying on the balcony of my wife's apartment where I passed out last night. It's three stories up and probably last night I was climbing the railing and playing Tarzan by hanging from the edge with one hand. My wife probably got bored and said to hell with him, and left me here. Too bad it didn't rain.

It's going to be a rotten day. The hangover is lying here with me just waiting for me to move. Now when I sit up with my back against the wall I feel the stuff in my throat coming up and I begin to gag. Nothing comes but a little phlegm that's almost black from all the cigarettes I smoked, but the dry heaves keep coming at me until it hurts like hell at the spot just past my asshole where my nuts start. It keeps coming and it scares me except I feel somewhere that this is all funny, but it keeps coming and I think I'm going to rupture myself just sitting there trying to puke. Things haven't changed a bit, I keep thinking. Christ, more than four years in prison and things haven't changed a bit. But I should be thankful, I try to tell myself. I should be thankful, I mean this is all so familiar. But I can't work up a laugh.

When I was young, I'm not that old now, only 29, but when I was really young like seven or eight, something like that, I first began to get this day-dream or fantasy about coming home. I was going to run away and become a famous jockey and then after ten years or so I'd drive home in my big Cadillac and my father would need money for his business and I'd give it to him, and I'd give beautiful and expensive gifts to my mother. When I was seven or eight I guess I began to notice people's remarks about how small I was and they said I should be a jockey when I got older and that's where I got the idea.

But when I got older the story didn't change except now I was going to be a world-champion boxer. I was going to run away and train for years in a secret cave in the woods and live off berries and wild animals and then one day I'd emerge and beat everybody in the ring because I was so strong and healthy and I'd become rich and famous overnight and then I'd drive home in my new Cadillac and . . . well, that part never changed. The idea came when I was about eleven and I went to the York Lions Police Club, where they taught boxing, except my mother found out one night when a boy hit me between the eyes and I fainted and they called my home.

Next I was going to be a rich and famous writer because in grade seven I wrote a composition about Hurricane Hazel that just about washed our house away. The water climbed all the way up the basement stairs and stopped halfway between where the last step was and the dining-room floor and my mother stood there crying and I thought for sure the water from her tears was going to be the thing that finally got us flooded out of house and home. The teacher thought it was so good that she sent it to *Liberty* magazine and they published it because they thought it was pretty good too, especially for a twelve-year-old and besides they had a special page where they printed stuff by students.

All my life that story has been in my mind and it was really funny because when the cops finally got me after that last bank and I was sitting in my mashed-up car against the stone wall of Casa Loma with the steering wheel jammed somehow in my chest and my head stuck through the broken windshield and me bleeding and the cop who was nervous and walked toward the car and saw me move and fired his gun and the bullet went through the door and into my leg, my mind made up two stories almost right away with me dying in one of them and everybody feeling really sorry because of course they blamed themselves; the other story had me in a hospital getting better very very slowly and everybody forgetting about me because when I got better I went to prison anyway, but then years later because I'd learned something really important that made me rich and famous, I drove to my parents' home in my new Cadillac and. . . .

The sun is beginning to form a line at the edge of the balcony. I can hear the kids upstairs in their bedroom throwing stuff around. I don't want to move from here. Ever. Just leave me alone here with this shakiness all pulled in tight, my legs up tight against my chest. If I don't have to move I can keep control.

I had $237 when I got on the bus. Money accumulated from making wallets and change purses over the past four years. Not exactly a fortune and certainly not enough for even a down payment on a Cadillac but I had plans for it. The $37 I was just going to blow, a bottle of champagne, a night on the town for Bernice and me. A hundred was for tools so I could get my old job back repairing cameras, the other hundred would go in the bank. I never was one for planning things much.

A fly is buzzing around my hair. Probably I stink. Fuck off, fly, I can't concentrate.

The balcony door opens, my younger daughter Lucy is standing there still in her pyjamas with the back flap open so you can see her behind, but still she manages to look sternly at me in a dignified way that makes me uncomfortable.

"Daddy, are you sick?" she says.

"Yes I am."

"Are you gonna go to bed?"

"No, I'm going to sit here until the sun comes and it'll melt me and I'll disappear."

She puts her thumb in her mouth and thinks about that for a few seconds, and then she decides (she is five, she decides quickly).

"No it won't. You're just making that up."

"You mean I'm telling a lie."

"Yes," she shouts gleefully and takes her thumb out of her mouth so I notice her front teeth jut out a bit, not badly, in fact it gives her mouth an attractive puffy look (in ten years the boys will compete to press their mouths against those lips). She points a finger at me, "You tole a lie."

"Before breakfast too," I say. I don't really want to talk. I have to think things out.

"Can I sit beside you?" she says.

"Sure, but you better close that back door or your ass'll get cold."

"Oh," she swings around indignantly and grabs at the flap. "Cathy was supposeta do that up."

She twists herself around and her eyes bulge with the effort of bringing the button and the hole together.

"Here, I'll do it."

"I can," she says but turns around anyway for me to do it. Then she sits down beside me, pulls her knees up tight against her chest and puts her hand in my lap, and I feel its damp warmth against my belly. It's the first time I noticed that my shirt is completely undone. It's a miracle I didn't catch a cold. Or something.

"Ya know what I'm gonna be when I grow up?" she says.

Oh shit, first thing in the morning.

"No, what're you going to be when you grow up?"

"A nurse!" she says. "An' then when you get sick ya won't haveta go to the hospital anymore. I can take care a ya."

I turn my head and look at her. She's a beautiful child, hair so blonde it's almost white and her mouth puffy like that and smiling proudly, even her eyes, which are blue like mine, have some kind of inner pride in them, like windows you can look right into her and see everything inside. They're always like that, her eyes, like windows with the sunshine just pouring into them and lighting everything up inside. Most people have curtains over their eyes. Or venetian blinds. It's funny looking into her eyes too because right between them she has a little blue mark, very small, and I don't know what it is or where it came from but I'm glad it's there especially after these past three days and the things that have happened between Bernice and me. And the mark makes me think of Deek, which makes me feel better, clearer, just thinking about him.

"That's really nice," I say to her and I reach to squeeze her hand, but she gets up.

"I'm gonna get dressed," she says.

And then she's gone.

The first fifteen minutes on the bus I had a lot of sex fantasies, partly about Bernice but mostly I just kept picturing pairs of tits that weren't attached to anybody, but real tits anyway, and crotches with hair on them that were hot and sweaty but not belonging to any particular body. It was easy to get a hard-on when I thought about those parts, bare asses kept wiggling through my mind, but it was frustrating too because I couldn't keep it up there when my mind wandered off trying to put together a whole figure with a face. I must have exhausted myself and I fell asleep.

When I woke we were in Toronto already and the first thing I did when I got out was to get a cab and go to the liquor store and buy a bottle of Mumm's champagne.

"Celebrating, eh?" the cab driver aid.

"Just got outa prison," I said.

"That right?"

"Yeah."

"Up Kingston way?"

"Yeah."

"How long they stick you away for?"

"Four years."

"That right! Geezus, ya kill somebody?"

"Nope, just robbed some banks."

It was perfect. He asked all the typical dumb questions and I sat there elated, like some returning hero.

"Didya use a gun?"

"Yeah."

"Didn't shoot anybody though?"

"Just one guy."

"Geezus, yer really lucky."

And that's how I felt. Really lucky. I didn't know why he said that to me, but I didn't question him. I didn't care what he meant, I felt really lucky.

He drove into the parking lot behind the address I'd given him. It was an apartment complex four stories high and when I got out of the car I saw Bernice up on the balcony of the third floor and she was waving. The kids were beside her waving too. They were shouting something but I couldn't make it out.

"The wife, eh?" my driver said.

"Yeah."

He looked up at her and for a crazy moment I thought he was going to wave too. My arms were flapping up and down and I must have looked like a religious fanatic to people in the other apartments. But I didn't care. I paid the driver, took the blue nylon bag the Institution had given me that contained two pairs of underwear, a pair of pyjamas, a rain-coat, three pairs of socks, a tooth-brush and a razor. Every-one got one when they left. I had a cardboard box too that had all my personal stuff like letters, mostly from Bernice, and my tools for making leather wallets and change purses. I got it all balanced with the bottle tight under my arm and started up the walkway.

"Have a good time," the driver called.

And when I looked up to where they were all still waving, I could see up my wife's dress and even though she was up really high I felt a hard-on coming, and I yelled back at the driver, "I will!" And as I walked to the elevator I was laughing at all the things the guy must be imagining.

I took the elevator up, tense inside myself, excited, nervous, expecting something but not knowing what. And I walked along the corridor for the first time. She was waiting at the door, wearing that look I remembered when she wasn't sure of something, a waiting look.

"Well, so here you are," she said.

"Yeah, I'm here."

Neither one of us giving an inch. And we stood looking at each other, examining I guess, like our faces were score-boards and the last four years had been a game and now both of us trying to figure out the score; see what side won. The silence was so long it made me feel like I was sixteen again in Carrot River, Saskatchewan selling magazine sub-scriptions from door to door, and in the middle of my pitch I forget the next line and the people are standing there waiting for me to finish and I can't think of anything to say, and I know it's no sale now but I can't even find words to get out.

"You look really good, Bernice," I said.

In the background there are two children, one's larger than the other. They're waiting for me to do something too but I can't even wave with my arms full. My mind searched frantically for the dial to turn on the sound, to move the projector from the still position and resume the action.

"Will ya please take this bloody bottle of champagne from me before I drop it, and stick it in the fridge so we can have a drink! Christ, I'm home. I wanna celebrate."

"I got one too!" she said. "And it's already cold."

And then like an explosion, she grabbed the bottle from me with one arm and the other stuff fell on the floor and her other arm swung around my neck and pulled me up against her mouth, and the two kids wrapped themselves around my legs and squeezed and pulled at me almost as hard as I did at the woman, my wife, Bernice. And for that small piece of time, I felt like a tree, pulled at, pulling, and these people around me made my base wide and my roots went deep. My arms were strong branches that could lift them all higher, closer to the sun.

Yeah, I came home after four years mumbling to myself like a goddamn poet. And I suppose this morning if I throw up my guts all over this balcony, this cement balcony reinforced with steel where nothing grows and even the gnats are skinny and have tired blood because there's nothing to eat but little pools of puke left by good samaritans like me, I suppose if I do that I'll call my vomit sap. The funny thing is everything started off well. Maybe I got my feelings mixed up with a Christmas tree.

"Geez, Joe," she said, and then her tongue shoved into my mouth again and my pants were bursting against the soft crush of her body. I felt like a snowman, my arms stiff, melting, my body losing its form, becoming a soft thing.

"You kids go out and play," she said.

I felt like a fish in water and their voices were like stones dropped from somewhere up above.

"You can talk to Daddy later," Bernice said.

She scraped them expertly from me, shuffled them out the door, locked it behind them, and then took my hand and led me in. I watched her undress, her face wearing that look my mother called bold.

"Com'on, you too," she said.

"God, your hair's really long," I said.

"You like?" and she twirled around until it swept out like a black cape that half hid her face. While she turned she unlooked her bra and teased my face by swooping low where I sat on the bed and passing her breasts inches from my mouth. I grabbed at her.

"Wait," she said, and pushed me onto the bed and began tugging at my pants.

"Oh, nice," she said and now it was her grabbing at me.

I tried to focus her face but it evaded me like the secret of a train station, a bus terminal where there's a feeling, a look, something that causes a stir inside you, but there are no details to explain, nothing specific to isolate the cause. I looked at the ridges of stretch marks on her breasts, the embossed lines on her belly that gave evidence of our children, and suddenly recognized the feeling in me; the feeling of hitch-hiking across the country to the west coast when I was fifteen and stopping at Sault Ste. Marie, Winnipeg, Saskatoon, Calgary, some of the smaller places and finally Vancouver, and in every place going to the train station or bus terminal to clean up, have a crap and then move on. There was always the feeling of being a stranger, which was exciting and couldn't be duplicated, but it was something that made you walk stiffly and turn your head sharp so it hurt if you happened to hear a name said loudly that was the same as yours.

"Joe," she said. "Come in to me."

I wanted to bury my head between her legs and with my tongue make her buck up and down until her legs strained into a bridge that lifted her behind up in the air off the bed and she laughed hysterically and whimpered like a kid, like Cathy used to do when I tickled her until she almost cried.

"Joe, come inside." And she caught hold of me with her strong hands and directed me between her legs where it was warm and wet and I kind of collapsed there as her hands moved to my ass and pulled me in tight, like she was putting on a shoe. And I felt weak and wonderful as she heaved her hips up and down, back and forth. My cock stiff inside her and my body, a paralyzed, electrified thing attached.

She unclamped her mouth from mine and I opened my eyes to see hers and there was hardly any colour in them, like they get when she's worried or in pain.

"Don't stop," she said.

But I wasn't doing anything except hanging onto the pillows at the top of the bed for some kind of safety. And I tried to think of something else to ease the tension that kept my body taut like a bow for each pull and release. But there was nowhere to go in my mind. I was here, and to get away I began to pump at her furiously until the final jerk when there is no control, the cleansing flood and then the calm when everything was okay again.

"Don't go," she said. "Just lie there fer a minute."

But I got up, feeling strangely restless. I lit a cigarette and lay down again.

"Are you glad you're home?" she said.

"Sure I'm glad, it's just. . . ."

"What?"

"I gotta get used to it."

Her hands were on me, running over my chest, going up and touching my face; they made me feel uncomfortable.

"Let's have a bath," I said.

"Together?" she said and smiled, her eyes with colour now.

"Yeah, like we used to." And I was up and running. I ran the bath and then went and got her bottle of cold champagne, a cheap brand I noticed and pink. She was in the tub with a flowered plastic thing on her head so her hair wouldn't get wet. It made her face look small.

"You look like a mouse with that thing on," I said.

"Smarty," she stuck out her thick tongue at me. "You wanna brush my hair if it gets wet?"

"No, no, keep it on. I don't mind havin' a bath with a mouse, especially such a cute one."

I ripped off the metal foil from the bottle and undid the wire holding in the cork, which was plastic. It hardly popped when I pulled it out and a little gas came up and went up my nose, my face was so close. I poured some of the stuff into the glass over the wash-basin, a plastic glass; I'd forgotten to bring some from the kitchen. I handed it to her.

"Where's yours?"

"We can both use that one."

It probably appealed to some romantic notion she had because she smiled again so wide I noticed the missing teeth from the back of her mouth.

"We should have a toast," she said.

"How about our undying love to the parole board who made all this possible."

I was trying to be funny, to keep it light, change the subject but her arm came up from the water and pulled me toward her.

"Joe," she said. "Joe, I love you."

I felt so sorry I could hardly lie.

"Me too baby. Me too," was all I could say. And her face was against my leg and she was crying and I felt awkward and embarrassed to have caused this but most of all not to be part of it.

And then when it was over for her we drank glass after glass of champagne until the bottle was almost gone and we got giddy and giggled and ignored the kids banging on the door. And we washed each other's back and made love again with her straddling me and laughing and me slapping her bum and saying, "Ah, nice rubber duck, nice rubber duck." And to make everything okay, she even quacked.

Later she left me to soak by myself while she got dressed and made the kids something to eat. I lay there half-drunk telling myself that everything was going to work out. I'd just have to work on it like Deek had said. Put some muscle into your marriage, he'd said, not those exact words but something like that. It made me laugh just thinking about it, instead of going to a marriage counsellor, you both join Vic Tanny's. But it was hard to keep it up when I remembered that we hadn't really told each other anything. Just got a little exercise together, I thought, and I tried to phrase it in my mind the way I would if I was telling Deek so I could make him grin and show the gold on his bad teeth. And then I remembered his word, flexible.

"You really aren't very flexible, Joseph," he'd said. "You have a way of demanding that things be exact and final. A little hard on other human beings, isn't it?"

Fuck you, Deek.

I lay soaking. Thinking.

My wife is older than I am by seven or eight years. I'm not exactly sure. I met her at a party when I was sixteen. I had the usual pimples, greasy duck-tail, white shirt with the collar turned up, draped strides and motor-cycle boots with chains on them. I bleached my hair blonde and thought of myself as pretty hot stuff, or cool, I can't remember what it was best to be in those days. It was hallowe'en, which was appropriate for the stage I was going through. People were out on the floor jiving and me and several other guys were circling the room like hunters surveying the game. She was off a bit by herself and I widened the circle to pass close by her and then probably smirking in my best Elvis Presley style, lip curled and all, I turned to my companion and said loudly, "Look at the tits on that." None of us had even got our laughs going when she reached out an arm, clamped a strong hand on my shoulder, spun me around and walloped me full in the face with her other hand.

"Shit, what the fuck are ya doin'?"

She swung again at me and I had to grab fast or I would have got it again.

"You nuts or somethin'?"

The other guys had moved off and were laughing.

"Let go my wrist or I'll let you have it again," she said. Her voice was deep, husky almost and she spoke through tight lips even though her mouth was soft looking, something you'd like to bite into. I let go.

"You always go around whacking guys?" I said.

"You always go around shooting off your filthy mouth?"

That made me really mad. I'd just come back from a nine-month stint on the road with a crew of guys selling magazines. We'd travelled the whole country, even the Atlantic provinces and I'd earned $110 a week, the highest of anybody in the crew, including Cass Stewart who'd come from Glace Bay. I knew how to use my mouth.

"You wanna dance?" I said. One thing, I could really dance.

"You know how?" And for the first time she smiled and it made her eyes crinkle and her mouth open to show small even white teeth, but there was something else that I couldn't see really, it was a feeling about her, she felt sad to me even though she was smiling and I liked that. It felt like something awful had happened to her but she wasn't going to bug anybody about it. She could handle it. There was a crazy kind of braveness about her that I liked because that was the way I felt about myself.

She danced better than I did but wasn't smart about it. She had a way of leading that was so smooth and easy to follow that anybody watching couldn't tell who was leading and they'd automatically assume it was the guy, me.

We didn't talk much except that she said she loved to dance and we danced together all night except when some guy would butt in but she always came back to where I was standing for the next one.

Her name was Bernice and when I admired the brown dress she was wearing she told me she had made it herself.

I told her my name and asked for her phone number which she gave me easily and then asked me for mine. I had the last dance with her and went home without even trying to kiss her. It has been a dreamy kind of night. I didn't feel the kind of excitement I usually did when I met a new girl. There were no fantasies in my mind about her on the streetcar going home. She had nice tits. I liked her long black hair, the

46

way it hung around her shoulders and then curled in to make the edge look round. I'd liked the feel of my arm fitting all the way around her waist, most girls were too big for me to do that. She was small like me and had brown eyes that could smile and a couple of times she'd winked at me from across the floor when she was dancing with someone else and that made me feel flushed and warm because no other girl had done that before. There was a toughness about her that I admired; the way she'd hit me, the way she led when we danced without seeming to, and her asking for my phone number like she was a guy. I kind of admired all that but it wasn't what I was used to. Going home on the streetcar I felt a calmness that I always figured older people must feel just because they're older, not all frantic and jumpy inside from always making new plans especially when it's got to do with a girl. Bernice was an experience. She made me think of the one time my father had taken me to a baseball game at Maple Leaf Stadium, the only real baseball game I ever saw in my life and I was really too young to know what was going on and fully enjoy it and in the eighth inning I had to go to the bathroom and he didn't want to leave so I went by myself and got lost so that by the time he found me we were the last people to leave the place and traffic was jammed. I decided there was something serious about Bernice to make me think of things like that.

When I got back to the boys' residence where I was staying one of the guys was in the hallway holding the phone.

"Fer you Cross. She's already called three times."

It was Bernice.

"I just got here," I said.

"I wanted to thank you," she said. "I don't like those parties and I never stay but I had fun tonight."

"Well, me too."

"An' I'm not sorry I hit you. You deserved it."

"Well, I'm glad you did. I mean I noticed ya, but I probably wouldn'ta got to meet ya if you hadn't done that."

"Because you're shy, eh?"

47

"Not shy exactly but sometimes it takes me a while to work up my nerve, ya know."

"I'll bet," she said and there was a soft teasing laugh in her voice. "Anyway, one of the girls here said there was going to be a hallowe'en party put on by the boys at your place tomorrow night."

"Yeah, there is," I said.

"I wouldn't mind coming if you take me," she said. "There's supposed to be dance prizes and I'll bet we could win them."

I was flattered but uneasy too. I'd only lived at the residence since I'd got back to town two weeks ago. I went to the party at the girls' residence where Bernice lived for laughs, something to do, but there were stories about the place; all the girls were a bit looney and had been in some kind of nuthouse before they came to live there. The guys might laugh at me if I invited one of them to our party.

She was waiting and I felt like I was being tested. I had to say yes. Shit, if anybody said anything, I'd say I was screwing her. She was good enough looking to make anybody's mouth water.

"What time should I pick you up?" I said.

"It's okay, I'll meetcha there."

She arrived half an hour after the party had started and just in time for the first dance contest. We won easily and she smiled and flung her black hair around like a prancing horse. The three prizes we won that night were all movie-theatre tickets and people started kidding us we'd have to go steady just to use them up. I was a bit bewildered by every-thing that was happening. Other guys from the residence were competing to dance with her, some of them a lot older than me and sometimes she danced with them, flashing her eyes at me in that teasing way that made me want to leave but she always returned to me and danced in the contests only with me. And then when I took her home she turned to me just before we reached the front door and without me asking or even making a move, she put her strong arms around me, pressed her mouth against mine and it was like

48

she plugged her tongue into my whole body the strange sensation I got, a kind of mild, pleasant shock that sent me home buzzing.

"I'll call ya," she said.

And she did but the whole thing was like a long-distance phone call: the next best thing to being there. I was dialled from faraway, talked to in pleasant words. I came home from work and there were messages for me: she loves you, yeah, yeah, yeah. But nobody had ever heard of the Beatles, not even Ringo Starr. I had a transistor radio with a little plug that fitted in my ear so I could listen to it on the streetcar without bothering anybody else and Canada's own Paul Anka whispered in my ear: I'm so young and you're so old, this my darling I've been told, but I don't care just what they say 'cause forever I will pray, you and I will be as free as the birds up in the trees, oh please stay by me. . . . And everything was smooth and romantic except in the dark if I got too close and slipped my hand up her leg, the receiver clamped down on my fingers and I was disconnected.

Her tongue was like a wire strung between us, a live wire with juice that got the message across. I dialled information more by mistake than anything else and learned what had happened.

She came from a good Catholic family. Stress the good, I never saw her pray once, even in the dark when I was eating popcorn, watching a movie and her mouth was empty. A large family. Fourteen kids and numerous shadows that resembled parents, father-figures I should say or more specifically sires. She was always a little vague on sexual details. But one day the recognized male figure in the parent bed did a finger count of those surrounding him at the breakfast table, recalled his adherence to the rhythm method and decided there was a Protestant in the woodpile. Not being an axe-murderer or even one for log-splitting, he just split. And of course that broke the whole family up.

A social worker reassured Bernice's mother and patted the child's eleven-year-old head. After all it was only temporary and the other children had to go to relatives' homes, not a nice cosy orphanage like Bernice.

It was a wooden place. The older kids got stiff on bootleg booze. I forgot to mention it was a small eastern Ontario town where there are no prejudices. And one of the juniors who was kept in a separate room decided to protest, a kind of strike, and he did it with a match.

After the fire, the social worker put Bernice and some of the other kids in her car and drove them to a huge place like a farm, all that space, those beautiful green lawns and lovely trees hanging low for shade. But there were bars on the windows and the waiters who served you, looked after you all wore white suits. And there were lots of nurses in case you got sick. Certainly some of the people sitting around on benches didn't look too well, the way they rested their heads between their knees and dribbled down their canes. It wasn't really disgusting and besides they had a special area for the children so you didn't have to be bothered by some old lady crapping in her drawers and playing in it until one of the nice waiters saw her and gave her hell. Yes it was a place for people who were . . . ah, disturbed, but after all there had been the fire and that was a pretty upsetting thing to happen to anybody so they could just stay there temporarily and rest.

She had a way of fitting in and twelve years later a distant relative going through the family album asked an embarrassing question about the little girl with black pig-tails who was soooo cute and kept appearing in early photographs but then suddenly disappeared. So a quiet letter of inquiry was written. It was received politely by an official and a week later Bernice was hustled into the hospital station-waggon and driven by a sunny-eyed, smiling, moist-handed social worker, a new one (the old one had become a patient), and they arrived in Toronto where Bernice was delivered to another kindly lady of the same order who ran a home for girls like Bernice who were considered "temporarily cured" by the hospital. It was a place where the girls could prove themselves.

Bernice of course was still a ward of the state. She had never been officially released, but now all she had to do was to work diligently for a year or two at domestic jobs selected for her by the social worker who ran the home. The home had a list of fine elegant women with beautiful homes, who were willing to give the girls a chance to prove themselves. And they even paid. The home was sent a cheque for $40 each month and the girls received $15 for spending money. If a girl walked to work, didn't smoke, shopped at the Salvation Army for clothes, by God in a year or two she could save as much as $100. And start a whole new life for herself.

It seemed kind of screwy to me and I couldn't understand it as anything but a long funny story or some kind of crazy joke. It didn't make real sense. In my mind it wasn't really real but I liked her. Even though she was older than me, her hands got hot and sweaty at the movies like mine. It was funny the way I respected her not letting me screw her. I figured she must be the oldest virgin in the world. Some kind of a saint. What it all meant then was that I didn't take her too seriously, especially when the week after I met her, I ran across a fifteen-year-old who lived in Regent Park, a huge housing complex where she was as popular as hell because of all the free baby-sitting she did for people, almost everynight in a different apartment. And she loved to screw. All I had to do was call her from work in the afternoon when she got home from school and find out where she was going to be that night. She even did it when she had the rags on.

Anyway, almost two months later it was Christmas Eve and Bernice had gone somewhere for a week, a brother had discovered her and took her home to decorate the tree or something. My little friend in Regent Park was tied up with her family, so I got together with a couple of older guys I hardly knew who hung around the poolroom near the residence where I lived, and after I bought six bottles of wine they dug up some girls and found a place for a party which wasn't too good because we got thrown out after an hour because we made too much noise. So we stood on the street, six of us, drunk, it was snowing, and some old guy was staggering toward us and stopped right in front where he had a car parked at the curb and when he got it unlocked and the key in the ignition, the two guys ran around to his door, hauled him out, punched him a couple of times and kicked him, and then jumped in his car. "Com'on," they said, and the girls and I did.

There was nowhere to go until I suggested my parents' cottage. I don't know why I thought of it. Maybe I wanted to contribute something. Everyone thought it was a great idea. And only a hundred miles.

We broke down the door by kicking at it. I tried to light the space-heater and it blew up. No-one got hurt but it made a hole in the wall. One of the guys found my brother's bow and arrow set and shot holes in the ceiling. We screwed the girls on top of my mother's satin spread and when I mentioned it was stained one of the girls laughed and cut out the stains with a knife. Before we left the girls loaded all my mother's cosmetics into an overnight case they found. And I helped the guys carry the portable TV and air-conditioner to the car.

The cops got us at St. Clair and Bathurst. It was Christmas morning, about 5 AM, and there was no traffic, and we were still a bit drunk and speeding and also on the wrong side of the road. And there was the thing about the car being stolen. The man had reported it after they got him to the hospital so it was logical they should stop us, but I guess we were all surprised when the two cops who stopped us walked toward our car with their guns out.

They put us together in one large room so we could talk. I thought the detectives at the station were friendly, there was a kind of weary concern about the way they asked where the stuff had come from. No-one would tell and they left us alone. But then the girls cried and confessed to me that they were on probation and when the guys turned to me I began to feel like a priest, yes they too had records and they would go to jail for sure unless. . . . Yes? Well, I was clean.

I'd probably just get a suspended sentence or at worst probation.

And suddenly I had this vision of me going to jail for a year or two and when I got out I stepped down from the train wearing a new suit, looking much older and carrying a suitcase filled with important papers and stories I'd written and I got a cab and had it take me to the restaurant where the guys and girls hung out. And of course they were waiting there for me and they greeted me by throwing their arms around me and shouting hurrah.

So I confessed and the detectives raised their eyebrows a little when I told how I'd knocked the old man down and kicked him.

The charges were car-theft, theft over $50, break and enter and assault causing bodily harm. It sounded impressive and when I signed the paper they let everybody else go.

The hardest part was an hour later they called me out and my father was standing behind the counter looking out the window to where it was snowing in the parking lot and his hair was wet because he'd forgotten to wear a hat. From the back I saw how thin his hair was, it got wet easily and the way it was glued down, it showed patches of his head underneath.

"Mr. Fair," the detective said.

And my father turned and I was surprised to see his face wasn't tight like it gets when he's angry, but slack like he was tired and his eyes looked dreamy, like I'd never seen them before. I couldn't figure out why he seemed so old until I noticed his cheeks looked sunken in and the most incredible thing I saw when he opened his mouth was that he had his teeth in. He only did that on very special occasions.

"Didya look at the stuff?" the detective asked.

"Yes."

"Is that it?"

"Looks like it." He shifted his look to me but it wasn't sharp and I didn't know if he even saw me. "Is this ours?" he asked.

"Yes, sir," I said.

"He'd know," my father said. "I can't remember, that looks like my wife's case and stuff and we've got a set at the cottage like that. The same kind of air-conditioner too, but I can't be sure. But he'd know."

"Well, we've just gotta check these things, Mr. Fair. Gotta have identification for evidence in court. If you just sign this."

My father bent over the piece of paper and I saw the lines in the back of his neck. I knew he probably couldn't read it, his eyes were getting bad. He looked at it for almost a minute, groped for a pen and the detective stuck one quickly in his hand and he signed. He continued to look at the paper.

"Does this mean we have to come to court?" he said.

"Oh no. Ya see we're laying the charge. This is just for evidence. You don't have to come near the court."

"Oh," my father said. And he turned his attention back outside to where it was snowing in the parking lot and I wondered if this year he'd finally bought snow-tires. He always claimed he never believed in them and every year there would be an argument with my mother about them.

I really wondered what he was thinking. And the detective was tapping the pen nervously on top of the counter. Everything was finished. All he had to do was go, but he stood there looking out the window, his back on a sideways angle to me so I could see one ear and part of his face. His mouth moved.

"Your mother got upset when they called. It was only a bit after six and we were sleeping so she got up to answer it. She thought it was her sister sick again. She was crying when I left." And then he paused for a few seconds. "I hope sometime you talk to her about this."

And then he left. I wondered if in a couple of hours he'd be standing beside the Christmas tree in the front room wearing his wine-coloured cardigan and brown baggy pants that seemed to get bigger and bigger because he got thinner and thinner, would he be standing there handing out presents? And would there be a box somewhere under the tree that contained a new flannel shirt for him? And what would he be thinking?

The trial was brief. I pleaded guilty and got two years less a day in the Ontario Reformatory. No-one I knew was at the trial.

In the reformatory I got along well. I was always good at following orders and after a couple of months they transferred me to a minimum-security institution that had modern forms of rehabilitation. I went to school half a day and the other half I spent learning how to be a tinsmith.

My friend in Regent Park wrote me letters and hinted she was pregnant, which made me kind of proud, but one day the social worker called me in and said he had a letter for me from a Bernice DeRoche which was ah . . . kind of romantic. Did I know a Bernice DeRoche? It took me a moment to put it together. I never had known Bernice's last name but when he told me the letter she'd sent was addressed to Joseph Fair and then in brackets Cross, I knew it was her. I'd told her my story too.

It was a hard letter to read. It was written in pencil, and the writing was small, the spelling was awful and phrases were turned around so they didn't make sense. I'd forgotten she'd told me she was French Canadian. She didn't have an accent and she spoke English fine but the first ten years of her life were spent in a small town just outside of Montreal. Farnham or something. So she wrote like a Frenchman because in the hospital there was no school for kids her age.

I figured out what she was saying. She blamed herself for me being in trouble as she called it. If only she hadn't gone away at Christmas none of this would have happened. I liked that kind of talk and I wrote her back and said I didn't blame her for anything and sure she could write and come and see me if she wanted. I'd like that.

She got one of the volunteers from the home to drive her up. The volunteer was a gorgeous blonde who drove a Cadillac convertible and when they drove up the road to the administration building every second Sunday, every guy in the place who could arrange it was out there, yelling and waving as they passed.

I spent blissful afternoons at the picnic tables they provided for visits in the summer with Bernice's thick tongue down my throat, her strong hand bending my shoulders toward the centre of my chest, and ten or twenty envious souls lurking behind windows and watching.

Naturally we agreed to get married when I got out. I was seventeen and I'd be eighteen by the time of my release. I say naturally because after a while there wasn't a lot to talk about and when we reached the stage where I talked about what I wanted to do with myself in the future, I said, settle down. And that meant marriage. Well, making plans for something like that can take up plenty of time and by the time my sentence was over we'd planned for six kids, a house in Scarborough, a cottage in Muskoka, two cars, one that I would teach her to drive. Even a fucking diaper service because it was cheaper in the long run, she said.

I got out and spent the first night with my friend in Regent Park. Luckily she had a baby-sitting job that night and the people stayed away until four. After that I alternated between her and Bernice. And I felt like a king when Bernice finally came across.

The details kind of get away from me after that. Bernice got pregnant about three months later. I asked her was she sure it was mine. My friend in Regent Park had taught me to be cautious after one night I took a friend with me just to meet her and ten minutes later she was screwing him too. Bernice started to cry when I said that and hung up the phone. I let her stew for a week but when I called the home they said she wasn't there and finally the woman who ran the place came on the phone and asked me to come in and see her.

"Bernice has gone back to the hospital," she said. "It's all for the best."

Two days later I got a letter from Bernice saying about the same thing. She was back at the hospital and they would take care of her and she didn't want to wreck my life.

That Friday night after work I got on the train and got to the town where the hospital was just in time for the senior staff to have left twenty minutes before. So I rented a hotel room that had a coil of rope next to the window in case there was a fire. And the next morning I was sitting in the administration building at nine o'clock, cooling my heels and waiting to see the superintendent.

Bernice knew I was there. Other girls had seen me and passed on the word. She sneaked away from her job to see me.

It was a large room with a high round ceiling. A rotunda. She saw me first because when I looked up she was watching me. There was a large distance between us. I couldn't see the details of her face. I saw her arms hanging loose, her hands open holding nothing. There was something about the way she stood, so unexpectant, that made me feel I could leave easily and never feel bad about it for a long time. But I couldn't stand the silence between us. I wouldn't lose her to silence. Like the guy I'd read about in prison. Orpheus. All he had to do was keep walking and this dame would follow but he couldn't stand the suspense so he looked back just to make sure and blew it. Didn't he know that not knowing, in the dark, in the silence, was the only way he'd ever really know anything?

I didn't know.

"Hello," I said. I almost had to yell, it was so far.

"Hello."

"I came to get you."

And she laughed and her arms spread out like wings in the echoing room and for an instant it seemed as if she would take flight and disappear into one of the corridors forever.

I moved toward her quickly, my heart and feet pounding hard. For a second I felt myself sink into something soft and then I began to run, one foot heavier than the other. And she was laughing loudly now. I knew I had to stop that. And then my arms were around her like rope, pulling her tightly against me.

"You crazy nut," she said between laughing. "You stepped in the wet cement."

Looking down, I saw one shoe was covered with the stuff.

So I rescued her. I guess you could say, with feet of clay. It seems funny now, sitting here on the balcony, my mind wandering back and forth, from here to there and back again to just a few days ago. None of it making much sense except that's the way things happened then so long ago and are still happening.

(And on the fourth day he created. . . .)

Yes the fourth day. Today is Monday. I'm supposed to look for a job today.

Already four days. Friday, drinking and screwing until I passed out in the tub. Saturday, the serious talk.

I woke up Saturday morning with someone beside me. It frightened me for a second. And I must have sat up with a jerk that moved the bed because she woke up kind of startled too. Four years being alone for both of us. It was something you got used to. A habit to grow out of again.

"I thought it was the kids," she said.

"I thought it was the screw."

We both laughed.

I noticed we both laughed when we were nervous.

"You have very good defence mechanisms, Joseph," Deek had said. "You can laugh at anything."

Almost.

"I don't remember getting here," I said.

"You didn't. You fell asleep in the bath and the kids and I carried you. Out like a light."

"Christ, I'm sorry."

"It's okay," and she leaned over, her hair falling over me and tickling my face. Her mouth was open to mine and I was annoyed because both our breaths were bad and I didn't want to start the day like that. I pulled away.

"What's the matter?"

"Just me," I said getting up. "I gotta brush my teeth. Can't stand my own stink."

She cupped a hand in front of her mouth, her eyes

squinted, her face serious like a child, and breathed out in short gasps.

"Mine's not so good either."

"It's just me," I said. "Just me." And I felt stupid, embarrassed and sad. Quickly I headed for the bathroom but she leaped out of bed and raced toward the door.

"Beatcha there!" she said.

And then I laughed and chased after her, grabbed her legs and tackled her. And while I was struggling to pin her arms down the kids' door opened and they were on top of us, screaming, pinching and tickling.

"Reinforcements!" I yelled when the three of them had me securely held down.

"Sssh," said Lucy. "We gotcha."

"What should we make him promise?" Bernice said.

"Notta go ta sleep in the bathtub!" Lucy said.

"Oh, silly," her sister said. "He was only drunk."

"Notta get drunk!"

"How about if I make breakfast?" I asked.

"Yeah!" Everybody yelled.

"Okay. Okay. I'm your slave."

They released me and I got up. This was what it meant not to be in prison. This was freedom. Their laughter like a breeze blowing me clean inside.

I scrambled eggs for everyone while they got dressed. It was nice to be doing something domestic like that. And briefly there was no-one around.

Bernice came down dressed and after washing her face seemed to be larger, her eyes set back farther so I had to look more closely, to get closer to see into them, and it made me feel that she could see me more clearly than I could her.

Later I announced I was going for a walk.

"Where?" said Bernice.

"I don't know. Just a walk."

"Can I come too?" Lucy asked.

Cathy didn't say anything. She was still playing with the egg on her plate, not watching but listening.

"Sure, you can all come. I thought I'd take a look around

the neighbourhood. Get the feel of the place. I see there's some beer empties. Take them back and get a dozen."

"You take the kids," Bernice said. "I'll do the dishes. You won't be that long, will ya? We could go shopping later."

Someone knocked on the door and Lucy ran and opened it. A little girl asked her to come out and play.

"I can't come," she said. "I'm goin' with my daddy!" And she slammed the door in the girl's face.

"Hey!" I said, "you shouldn't do that."

"She always does it," Cathy said.

There was no time to stop and ask, What's wrong Cathy? Why are you so quiet. Why I remember when you couldn't be shut up. I used to love to listen to you. How come you're so skinny? And old? And bitter?

We walked through the apartment complex down to Queen Street. It was only a couple of blocks but it made me feel strange. Two days before I'd been walking in the exercise yard. The same hot sun shone down. It was late August and in prison that meant a quiet time. It was too hot to do anything. A few guys jogged and there were some who played scrub ball but mostly guys tried to find some shade and lie down. Get away from the sun burning through the numbness. But here the streets were jammed with life that bounced and jostled against you so it couldn't be denied. Kids like swarms of insects buzzed around my legs. Kids wet from the wading pool wearing shorts with big safety-pins in them to keep them up brushed against me and asked the girls, "Who's that guy?"

"My dad!" Lucy said.

"Our father," said Cathy, her tone implying, What a stupid question.

But it was a public-housing project so maybe not many of the kids had fathers that were too evident. Abandoned wives. Unwed mothers. Wives waiting for their husbands in prison.

It made me feel good to be walking along with the kids like that. I felt like some kind of status symbol. But worried too because I hadn't figured out where I was in all this. What was going to happen?

Queen Street made me nervous. All those people rushing around. Going places. Doing things. Everything with a purpose. A direction. Well, Monday, I thought. Monday I'll be okay. I'll get a job and know what's happening. In the meantime, just relax.

I found the beer store and cashed in the bottles.

"Get Red Cap!" Lucy said.

"What?" I was surprised.

"Tony gets that," she said.

"Who's Tony?"

"He's nobody," Lucy said. "He comes around some-times."

Nobody who comes to visit sometimes. Everything inside of me tensed up.

"He's really nobody," Cathy said, and Lucy's face was like a candle suddenly extinguished, no light, no flicker, a darkness I didn't know.

I bought a case of beer, not Red Cap, and on the way back picked up a bottle of whisky and two more of wine. My supplies, I thought.

"Can we go to the zoo?" Cathy asked.

"Yeah, I wanna come too," Lucy said.

"Sure, why not?" It seemed appropriate that my first full day out should be spent at a zoo.

Bernice watched me put the beer and liquor away.

"Gettin' ready for a long winter?"

"Just like to have it around in case I want it."

"I'm only kiddin'." Her arms around me suddenly and her tongue inside my mouth holding back the words, the questions.

"Let's send the kids outside. . . ." Her body demanding my attention but a crazy feeling in me that we are each split into two parts: the horny part of me, the horny part of her scrambling for satisfaction, but it makes me think of the couplings on box-cars. The couplings can come together and interlock and that's their mission in life, but what about the box-cars. It doesn't matter to them what's inside the box-cars.

"I promised the kids to take them to the zoo. You wanna come?"

"You're just scared of me." She's teasing me but in a way she's right. Everything here frightens me. It seems so easy to break but that's not right either. It's like getting angry at a stranger in a bar and picking up an empty beer bottle and smashing it against the table to break it and scare him and finding your hand bleeding and full of broken glass.

"Will you come?" I asked.

"Sure. What should I wear?"

"Whatcha got on. You look great. Beautiful."

"Really? I feel so old sometimes. Sometimes at nights I feel like I'm going to die, I feel so old."

Her arms around me again. Crying into my shoulder, heaving, in a way almost like a wet dog shaking off the water, the stiffness leaving her until she's soft against me and my own body is stiff but bent in toward her.

"I'm so glad you're back," she said. "So glad. I love you."

"I care about you too." I said. I hoped I wouldn't have to explain myself.

The kids were playing in the open-air corridor that runs along the floor of each building.

"Here they come!" Lucy shouted to the girls she was playing with. "My mommy and daddy."

It was only a short walk to the zoo and when we got there we split up in pairs.

"I wanna see the monkeys!" Lucy said.

"They're dumb," Cathy said.

"What do you want to do?" I asked.

"The bear. The white one."

"The polar bear."

"Yeah."

"Okay," I said. "You and I'll go there and we'll meet you guys later. Okay?"

"Sure," Bernice said. "Com'on little monkeyface."

We stood watching the bear for a long time. His pool of

water was full of debris, crap people had thrown in, popsicle sticks, potato-chip bags and the pool itself had a shiny green look to it. Sometimes the bear would raise himself to snatch at a thrown peanut but most of the time he sat on his haunches, his back against the wall, and stared between his legs.

"How come you like him best?" I asked.

"I don't like him best. He's stupid!"

"Why?"

"If I were him, I'd climb over the fence and escape."

"That'd be pretty hard to do. The fence is curved down like that so he can't."

"I'd figure a way."

"But how come you figure he's stupid when all the other animals are caged up too and they don't escape?"

"I don't know," she said.

It was a crazy argument to be having with a kid just eleven but there was something in it that I wanted to know. I had the crazy feeling she could tell me something about myself. About the confusion inside of me.

"He should know better than the others," she said. "He's bigger and smarter."

"But you said he was stupid."

"I mean because he stays there."

"Sometimes you don't have any choice," I said. It seemed like a stupid comment but I was beginning to feel uncomfortable, like trying to put together a jig-saw puzzle without having the cover of the box with the picture that showed you what the final thing was supposed to be.

"Let's go get some popcorn," I said.

"All right. Can we come back and feed some to the bear?"

"If you want."

It hasn't always been like this. Five years ago. Christmas Eve. We were going to have a party. Bernice began to hemorrhage. The woman downstairs watched Cathy while I drove Bernice to the hospital. Not to worry, the doctors said. It's not a miscarriage. You got here in time. We'll have to keep your wife a few days though. And back home

63

people showing up. Gene and Betty arriving as I come in the door. Is everything okay? You look frazzled, man. Hey, I brought along some great stuff. One joint and you're flyin'. Everything okay, man? Yeah, everything's cool. And Cathy asking: is Mommy all right? Is her baby okay? Sure. Sure, baby, everything's fine. And later when the place was jammed and we all sat and watched as she opened her presents, smiling at us all, still wearing her ruffled party dress at two or three in the morning because I'd forgotten she was waiting to open the presents and all of us stoned, smoking and drinking, trying to blow the tops of our heads off so something inside could escape, leave us alone, and her, sitting in the middle of us as the joint was passed around opening her presents, smiling and passing them around so everyone could see and feel them. From my dad, she said. No talk of Santa Claus. A queen reigning over us. Caring for us. Passing to Gene and Lou the electric hockey game I'd bought her and showing them how to put the batteries in and sitting with them till it was beginning to get light as they played violently, tipping the board, throwing the puck at each other and her laughter making it okay. Everything was fine. Finding napkins after the bootlegger had left for the second time and the pickin' chicken had arrived. Smiling always smiling. Holding my hand sometimes and changing the records. And then looking dizzy and worn down but still smiling until she fell asleep in my lap.

It may have been the instant that afternoon when she walked into the bedroom where I was passed out with Ellie and she shook me until I woke up and asked me, Why are you sleeping with that woman?

Now it feels, sitting beside her on this bench, that she doesn't trust me anymore. Everything's no longer okay or fine or even all right.

Never try to experience something over again. I told myself. There's no such thing and no such word. Remembering is bad enough. Even doctors are reluctant to do surgery on the same spot twice.

"Let's go see your bear," I said.

64

"Okay."

He was still sitting there, his head down.

"Maybe he's sleeping," I said.

"No, he doesn't want to see anybody."

"Well, I've felt like that lots of times."

"Me too," she said.

"It goes away."

"Sometimes."

"Do you read much?" I asked.

"Not too much. I like to watch TV."

"There was this book I read when I was away, about a man who went away from his home to fight in a war."

"Uh huh."

"Well see, it was a really big war with thousands and thousands of men fighting but most of the time they didn't get to see each other. They fired bombs at each other from miles away and sometimes men got killed but you never knew who did it because you couldn't see them. So this man spent the whole war loading bombs and rockets in big guns and he never once saw who they were being fired at. And then one day after many men were killed and years had passed someone came and said the war was over, the side he'd been fighting for had won. And so he went home. . . ."

"And lived happily ever. . . ."

"No!" I said. "No, he didn't. See, he was a fisherman and he had a small house by the sea. And he had a wife and a son. And every day he used to go out in his boat and fish and when his son got old enough he was going to teach him how to fish. But when he got home after so many years, the house was empty. There was a note from his wife saying she had to go to the city to find work and she would write him and let him know where she was. But the note was covered with dust so it was written a long time ago and he searched the house but couldn't find any letter.

The mailman came by every second day in a boat. The man lived on an island and that's the only way the mail could be delivered to the people that lived there. The first time the man saw the mailman he asked if he had a letter. The mailman was surprised to see the man. He told him he'd heard that he'd been killed in the war. Well the man said he hadn't and now he was home for good and was there any mail for him. And there wasn't.

Well it went on like that for years. Every second day asking for mail and there never was any. So the man fished and lived like he always had but it got harder and harder for him to keep his mind on things without his wife and boy waiting at home like they always had.

One day the mailman brought him a newspaper with a picture in it of a man who was a hero in the war. He was a hero for the side that had lost the war and had been hiding because he was scared if people found out what he'd done they'd want to punish him. But now he said in the story he wasn't ashamed anymore."

"Ashamed of what?"

"Of what he'd done in the war. All the people he killed."

"But he couldn't see them anyway. You said that."

"Yes, but. . . ."

"So what happened?"

"The fisherman hated the man in the picture. He blamed him for everything that was wrong with his life."

"Why did he do that?"

"Because he needed someone to blame. Just like when you don't do your homework and you blame the dog or your sister for ripping your book. You know."

She grinned. Dimples in her thin cheeks. Hidden. Her eyes, brown like her mother's, flashing as if they contained pivoted silver spinners some secret wind has blown. Like fishing lures trolling just below the surface of the water, her eyes and me watching, ready to snatch greedily at the bait, to be hooked and pulled up from wherever I am. Wherever I am.

Her long hair, half-way between the colour of mine and Bernice's, hanging there so gently, like a net. To catch me or to catch me?

"I did that sometimes," she said.

66

"We all have, I guess."

"Did he want to hurt the man?"

"He wanted to find him and kill him. So he cut out the picture and got in his boat and headed out across the ocean to find him."

She watched me carefully, wary, but listened.

"He searched everywhere for the man. The paper hadn't given an address so the man kept having to ask people to help him. He showed them the picture from the newspaper but no-one had seen the man. People asked him why he was searching for the man and he told them a lie. He said the man was an old friend. And the people were all sorry they couldn't help. They gave the fisherman food and let him sleep in their spare room. And after a while the picture from the newspaper began to get faded from so many people handling it and then the fisherman did a strange thing. He began to show people the photograph of his wife and son instead."

"Why did he do that?"

"Because I guess that's who he really wanted to find."

"Why didn't he say that?"

"I don't know, Cathy."

"Did he ever find them?"

"In a way, yes. You see the search had taken years and years and people were so friendly to the fisherman he spent more and more time in one place and he began to care less about finding the man and killing him. He still fished and one day he had a huge catch and decided to take the fish into the nearest city and sell the ones he didn't need. So while he was there and had the money he thought he'd buy some presents for the people who treated him so kindly and tried to help him and while he was doing that a man walked by with a woman and a boy that the fisherman recognized."

"The fisherman's wife and his son, right?"

"Right," I said. "And it was the man whose picture was in the newspaper they were walking with and they were all smiling. The boy was almost a young man now and the woman was older than his wife had been but he knew it was them."

"Did he say hello?"

"No, he didn't say anything. Just smiled as they walked by, they looked so happy and made him feel the same way but there was something about the man's face that bothered him. It was like the newspaper picture, which he still had, and when he got outside he took it out and looked at it over again. He looked at it for a long time and knew there was something wrong and when he looked up at the glass in the store window he saw a reflection of himself and the face he saw in the reflection was the same as the one on the man who had passed him with his wife and son."

"What did he do then?"

"He didn't do anything. There was nothing to do. Just that he felt glad. And then he got in his boat and went home."

"Home to the island?"

"No. You see, the thing was that wasn't his home anymore. He went back with his presents to the people who'd been nice to him."

"That's like a fairy story," she said.

"In a way, yeah." My mind was busy trying to understand why I'd thought of it. It wasn't something you just began thinking about. It came from somewhere.

"Sometimes they tell us stories like that at Sunday school," she said.

"You go to Sunday school!" I was laughing.

She grinned and flicked her hair around so the back of her head faced me.

"Sure, sometimes. They got a bus to pick you up."

"Hey! I just thought of it," I said. "The bear. The fucking bear. Right there," I said pointing down. "He made me think of it."

"What, Daddy?"

"The story. When you were talking about him that's what you made me think of. That story."

"He's different from the story."

68

"Yeah, I know." I knew he was. But I'd wanted to tell her I understood about the bear. How she felt. I wanted her to trust me again.

"I hope we can have fun together again," I said. "'Member how we used to?"

Her face turned back to me for an instant and then she pressed it against the bars of the bear's cage and her voice was muffled, faraway.

"Sometimes I 'member we useta."

And I grabbed her slender body, put my head down quickly and scooped her up on my shoulders and began to run. And her legs squeezed in tight to my sides, her warm hands cupped under my chin, her small behind thumping against my back, and she was yelling, whooping and laughing. She was laughing.

"I'm gonna lassoo the giraffe!" she yelled. "I'm as big as the giraffe. Noooo body can catch us. We're gonna flyyyy."

Too quickly I was tired. She was heavier now. I stopped and put her down. We were both panting. We looked at each other. There was nothing to say. It was better for now, I felt. I felt better anyway.

"We'd better find the others," I said.

She hesitated for a second, took my hand and began to skip along with her long thin legs. I couldn't keep up and began to skip too. And then she stopped.

"Can we come back here sometime?" she asked.

"Sure," I said. "Sure. Anytime."

It was August. Hot and sticky outside. My second day out of prison. And inside me it felt like Christmas.

When we got back to the apartment I poured myself a glass of wine and put some ginger ale in it. A stabilizer. There was still a lot left to the day. Bernice went shopping with the kids and I got tools and leather out. Thought I'd make a purse. I couldn't find a table that was right though. Or the lighting. In prison each cell had a desk that was perfect for working at, reading, leather-craft, anything. It was just the right height and had a surface that was like cork and you didn't have to worry about scratching it up. And

69

the lighting had been designed to be just right so your eyes didn't get strained and you could see what you were doing.

I took another drink to the living-room and opened the curtain so I could see out at the kids playing in the parking lot. It amazed me how they didn't get killed the way they weaved in and out of the moving traffic, like some complicated electronic game with lights flashing, figures on a board moving, numbers coming up and nothing, to an outsider anyway, seeming to have any order.

It was cooler in the apartment and the alcohol had made me feel comfortable and secure. It was just nice to sit there alone and the chair was deep and soft. One of the chief complaints in prison to do with cell design had been the chair that came with the desk. The chairs were that metal fold-up kind you see at church socials or bingos. Hard as hell on your ass after a while. I used to take the pillow from my bed and use it as a cushion. Then it wasn't so bad. Still not as good as this though.

My mind drifted. I didn't want to do anything but this. Sit there a little high, things blurred a bit and in my own time bring everything into focus. Otherwise, I thought the whole picture would be ruined by over-exposure.

And then they were back and I was helping them in the door with the bags. And the kids seeing the leather stuff asking me if I'll make then new purses. Sure. Sure. And another drink while I showed them how to cut out small patterns on scraps of leather.

By supper everything was nice and hazy. I sat with my fourth drink while they ate.

"Your meal's getting cold," Bernice said.

"I'm not hungry. Me and Cathy ate a bunch of popcorn at the zoo and it killed my appetite." I grinned over at the kid but she was looking down at her plate.

Later Bernice sent the kids out to play while she did the dishes. I remained at the table with my drink and pulled back the curtain so I could see out the window. More kids. Like a disease. A small army that out-numbered us three to one if they ever wanted to take over. A result of over-indulgence by the poor in their limited leisure-time activities. Alka seltzer for the middle-class and kids for the poor. Middle-class people don't have kids, they have children. Poor people have kids. But poor people screw and the middle-class make love. Probably rich people fuck.

"Joe, I wish you wouldn't do that," Bernice said.

"What?"

"If you're not going to eat supper, tell me ahead so I don't put out food or go away somewhere. I have a hard enough time trying to get them to eat as it is."

"I wasn't hungry. So big deal."

"It is a big deal!"

"So I'll eat in my room. I'm used to that anyway."

"Have you looked at those kids!" She was yelling. It was giving me a headache, making me come back.

"Sure, I know what you mean. They're both pretty skinny."

"Skinny! I've had Cathy to the hospital at least once a month. The latest thing is a heart murmur. And Lucy. . . ."

"Okay! Okay, so they need to eat and I'm not helping out by sitting here setting a bad example. I get the message, Bernice. Now get off my back."

"Get off your back!" The tears in her eyes frozen into ice. And then her voice softer, a sharper knife. "Get off your back, Joe, you haven't been here!"

That's right lady, I haven't. Don't tell me your past troubles and sorrows. I've got my own.

"I know it's been hard," I said. "I don't want to make it harder." And inside I felt that was right. I meant that. And there was the possibility that I might.

"Oh, let's not fight," she said.

"I don't mind."

I went into the living-room and put all my leather things away. Tomorrow, I thought, I'll get an early start and do something, but still it made me feel depressed to have done nothing when one of my plans was to start in on it first chance so I'd have some things to sell. I felt a restlessness to

71

produce something. I went out and got another drink and this time brought back the bottle. From somewhere far away I heard Bernice calling the children.

"Cathy, Lucy! Bedtime!"

It was getting dark again. Almost another day gone. Nothing bad had happened. Some good things but nothing really bad. Funny I keep expecting that. Always on my guard against it as if inside of me there awaits another mouth that will suddenly begin to speak, tell lies, curse people, bit and spit at them. My own mouth clamped shut and only able to open later when the damage has been done and say, I'm sorry.

There's really not a hell of a lot to do. I flick on the TV. Back in the joint guys are watching TV too. Saturday night. They get to watch the late show. But I get my choice of channel. No votes unless Bernice and I disagree.

Noise upstairs. Kids getting ready for bed, fighting with each other. Why do people get noisy just before they go to bed? Kids and prison inmates. On the range after a late show guys would be coming back to their cells and yelling and screaming at each other, waking me up, until I pounded on the door or threw the chair. And them laughing.

"Goodnight, Daddy."

Cathy's arms around me kissing my mouth gently. Taste the toothpaste. Does she taste the wine?

"Goodnight, kid."

"Don' gota sleep in the bathtub," Lucy says. And hugs me.

"I won't. Don't let the bed-bugs bite."

"I wanna horsy up to bed," she says.

So I oblige her, down on all fours, Lucy on my neck and Cathy on my back.

"That's a pretty big cliff for the horse," I say at the stairs.

"Com'on horsy!" And Lucy kicks her heels into my ribs. Seen too many westerns. Faithful old horse always comes through in a pinch.

So I plod up each step, my arms aching, both of them jumping and heaving on my back, knowing tomorrow I'm going to feel this but worrying that one of them might fall backward, crack open her skull. . . . Jesus Christ. Being the son is easier than being the father.

"Joe, don't hurt yourself," Bernice says.

And then collapsing on their bed and being quickly covered by the quilt and changing from horse to captive.

"Com'on you guys," I say in my best chief-keeper tone. "Into bed on the double." And watching both their faces change from the wideness of joy and excitement to the shrunken shape of obedience. Like accordions being stored away by their owners who still want to make music.

I kissed them and put out the light.

"Don't close the door," Cathy said.

"Won't the light in the hall bother you?"

"No."

Why is she frightened of the dark?

My bottle waits.

Bernice is watching TV, her face intent, leaning forward to catch every image, every sound. Her mouth is slack as if there's nothing for her to ask or answer. I guess maybe that's why I dislike TV. It makes you look and feel like that.

"Wanna drink?" I ask.

"Are they okay?"

"Sure, all settled in." I pour myself one and kill the bottle. I'm remarkably clear headed, I thought, and that made me feel good. Justified. See, all I needed to do was relax.

"Have you thought about what we're going to do?" she said.

"About what?"

"Everything I guess. Job, money, us. Do you want to stay living here?"

"It's okay until we get better established. I mean the rent's cheap. We couldn't do better than that."

"They'll probably raise it now."

"Why?"

"If you get a job, I mean."

"Well, I'll get a job, don't worry about that. Monday.

73

I've got some letters to see people I arranged in the joint. I might even get my old job back. I wrote them too and they said to come and see them when I got out."

"I'm not worried about a job, Joe. You were always good at that, it's what we're going to do. Our plans."

"I plan to have another little smash a this stuff. Want some?"

"Okay, a small one."

In the kitchen when I open the refrigerator I'm surprised to see how little food there is. I start opening cupboards and they don't hold a hell of a lot more. Lots of Kraft dinner, spaghetti, macaroni. Crap. And we used to complain in the joint because they fed us too much roast beef.

Shit! Roast beef AGAIN!

Yeah well, it hurts to see that kind of habit. Now I guess it is a habit, buying that way because there's not much money and it makes me think of how I complained about her not coming to see me and her trying to explain about the mother's allowance cheque that didn't include $30 travelling expenses for the once-a-month visit. So in four years she came twice but now I wonder what it really cost her those times. Yeah it hurts because someone's got to take the blame and society doesn't have a face or a phone number. And now she wants to make plans. And all I feel is, how am I going to be able to make this all up to them?

She's slouched forward even more now. Maybe she needs glasses.

"Here," I said and handed her the drink.

The room is dark except for the light from the TV. The sound is turned low so the kids can get to sleep, I guess. A movie is playing and it seems strange for Bernice to be trying to follow it and making plans at the same time. The movie is a romance with Ava Gardner so maybe it's not. I don't recognize the male hero. I'm sure his mother wouldn't either.

"I was thinking," I said, "that probably we'd stay here a while and see what happens with me and the job situation. I should be getting $150 a week to start if I'm repairing

74

cameras again. Then we stash a little away and when we've got some saved then we move."

She talked without looking away from the screen.

"I was wondering more about us. The kids are used to the school around here. I'm used to it too. That's not the big thing."

"It's a lousy neighbourhood," I said, ashamed that I said it, they had no choice, and ashamed that they'd had to live here, that they'd had no choice.

"How do you feel . . ." she said, now looking at me, her face lit by the grey light so she looked like she was made of stone, shiny grey like marble, no lines or scars. Perfect in a way but remote. "About us?"

"Okay. Nervous. I said that before. I'm nervous about everything."

"It's just there was so much happened and we never really talked in our letters about what was going to happen to us when you got out. A lot of times I thought you weren't coming home."

"I said a lot of things. I got mad. You didn't come."

"I couldn't."

"Yeah, I know." I said. Now I knew. I understood. I didn't want to dwell on it. To think about it all.

"Well, that's all done," I said. "We've got a whole. . . ." And I finished off my drink, my throat suddenly dry. "A whole fuckin' life ahead. We can have good times."

"I've had good times," she said.

"Yeah." And I suddenly thought of Tony. Good-time Tony. I was getting high. "Lucy told me," I said.

"What?"

"About the good times. Good-time Tony!" Why was I saying this crap? It didn't matter at all unless I wanted to avoid the real thing. Of being scared.

"I told you I went out," she said. Her voice had risen and she'd turned back to the screen. She didn't want to talk about that either. It wasn't important to us.

"I'm sorry. I'm just feeling . . . pushed Bernice. Hedged

75

in. You know what I mean? I mean I don't know what to tell you. I'm willing to try. Okay. I wanna try."

I got up quickly and went back to the kitchen for the other bottle. I was all soft inside, my throat hurting as if I'd screamed for a long time. Or had wanted to.

She was waiting, facing the doorway. "I'm sorry too," she said. "I don't want you to feel pushed by me. Or boxed in. I get scared seeing you drink. I wonder what's going to happen. I don't want it to be like it used to be."

How did it use to be? Right now I can hardly remember and isn't that good? I mean it doesn't matter anymore.

"It wasn't all bad," I said.

"I know."

She watches me in the dark. What does she see? I feel like a ghost who could drift away, like I'm made of clouds the wind could blow away or change the shape of. What shape am I tonight to her watching me? Inside I'm okay. That doesn't change but she can't see that.

"Do you love me?" she asked. "Us. The kids and me? Because that's all that matters, you know. I mean I don't care about other things, Joe, but I want to know. . . ."

"Christ, Bernice I'm home. I'm here because I care about you all. I have . . . trouble with the other. I mean I'm not even sure what it means. I care about you."

Her hands are moving in the dark. All I have to do is hold them. Loving and being loved is having someone to take your hand when it feels alone.

"I'm sorry Joe. I didn't mean to . . . to push you. I get scared sometimes. I can't. . . ."

She's crying, softly, her face away from me so I can't see it, but I know. She's cried alone a lot, I guess. While I was away. She's a stronger person now than before. I can see that. So am I.

I pour another drink, my mind drifting off. Something inside falling.

I fell asleep I guess. When I woke up, the TV was off and the room was dark and becoming cold. I went up to bed and Bernice was asleep. I didn't wake her.

76

I'm twelve years old. Last June I received a bicycle for passing out of public school. That year I got the strap sixteen times for writing too small. I wondered why the teacher didn't wear glasses. An ex-army man, he probably thought they'd be unmasculine. Someday he'll be blind. I see him sitting in the dark clapping his hands together for some noise to fill the emptiness.

I still write small but my hands are tougher and I've learned how to make a fist. I'm learning to be measured by how hard I hit back.

I try not to start things.

My mother sent me to register for the first day of high school wearing short pants.

I carry a fish-knife in my pocket with a piece of coat hanger fitted into it to make a spring. An older boy showed me how. It gives me six more inches to fight with. I notice though that most people don't want to fight when they think they might get hurt. I don't mind though. I'm used to it, so I win more often now with threats. The silent kind are the best.

I have a job after school delivering for a drugstore. I work Friday nights late and all day Saturday and Sunday. It keeps me away from the house.

Also I have a brother. He's two years old.

I think a lot about my brother. Most nights after the long bus ride home from school. I go to a special trade school because my last teacher in public school told my parents I was too stupid to go to normal high school My concentration span is limited, he said, and he was right. He bored me. Most nights I come home to get my bicycle to go to work and my brother is in the backyard playing in his wooden pen.

He recognizes me.

"Joe, Joe," he says, but its like Yo, Yo. And he raises his arms for me to come and lift him.

I try to get there every day with enough time to do it. It's hard to explain how it makes me feel to pick him up and carry him around for a few minutes. I like to go to the part of the backyard that's hidden from the house by the garage. Then I sit down with my back to the garage and bounce him on my knee and talk while he mostly laughs.

In a way it's like he's my son. Not my real son like I was his real father, but like I'd adopted him.

"And in eight or ten years," I say, "we'll be able to go fishing. You'll like fishing, feeling the thing pull on your line and pulling it, your heart all excited. And if it's too big, I'll have the net to help you.

And we'll go camping. I'll make us a tent out of clear plastic like the cleaners use and it'll keep out the bugs and mosquitoes, but at night we'll be able to lie there and see out at the moon and stars.

I'll teach you how to ride my bicycle too and maybe you could get a job in the same store and we could work together.

He sits bouncing on my knee and laughing but it's not how other people laugh to make fun of you. He laughs like he's happy.

Once my mother caught me talking to him like that. She said I was crazy and I think she told my father. He didn't say anything though. Maybe he understood I wasn't trying to do anything that would hurt anybody. There was nothing wrong with it. He was my brother.

My mother doesn't trust me very much. She's always reminding me of things I know I have to do. Feed the dog. Clean up his papers. Take him for a walk. Do my homework. Have a bath.

I wonder if my mother knows I don't trust her for thinking I'm stupid.

It's hard to tell about my father. He never says much. I think he's disappointed about something and it makes him not trust anybody.

Because he's so small and helpless and never turns from me when I'm around but puts out his arms for me to hold him, I feel like my brother trusts me.

I think about that when I'm delivering prescriptions, some of them worth a lot of money and important because the person waiting for them is very sick and needs it badly. The people waiting trust me. And Al who owns the drugstore trusts me too. But neither one has much choice once I leave the store. I could pedal my bike anywhere and they'd never see me again. The thing is neither the customer nor Al would be surprised. They'd each find an excuse for me being a shit. For me, that's not really being trusted. I mean, neither one of them could be hurt by me.

I work from five to eight school nights so I'm never home for supper. I grab a hamburger or hot dog at the restaurant next door. I take a bottle of pop from the cooler and go into the back room and eat by myself. I like it that way. Al does the same thing and he's married with three kids.

I enjoy it when I get paid and can buy things. My mother likes those fancy compacts or what Al calls purse perfumes, a small bottle of the stuff inside a fancy gold container. I usually get her something once a month and Al gives me a discount. He knows my mother doesn't like me working there but the presents keep her mind off it.

I like to buy new brands of cigarettes for my father. Every week I give him a pack of something different. Matinee, DuMaurier, even American cigarettes like Winston. I'm not sure if he smokes them, but he thanks me.

My brother's too young to buy anything for yet so I always save part of my money for when he's bigger. And I take him for walks in his carriage when I can. My mother is always nervous about this.

It's still fall when I'm twelve. When it's winter I'll be thirteen. A teen-ager, my mother says. I don't know what difference that'll make. I already have pimples and even the stuff Al gives me doesn't help.

The fall is a bad time for my mother for some reason. Maybe because we have to come back from the cottage and not go to the wiener roasts, the bingos and dances at Saba Beach. She misses that, I think. She seems to have more friends there. People like her better. Even I do. In the winter there's not much for her to do and I wonder if sometime she isn't lonesome for the cottage and summer.

Yom Kippur is in the fall and Al who is Jewish closes his store. So I get a whole night off and ask to take my brother for a walk. I know he likes to go out in his carriage but for some reason my mother rarely takes him.

She gives me permission and tucks him in with an extra blanket and warns me to be careful.

I push him up our street, past the houses where I know who lives inside to where I don't know anybody so we're both even. And he laughs and kicks off his blanket to play with his feet.

I take him up Dufferin Street, which is busy now because of rush-hour. And then we end up in the yard of my public school. Someday you'll have to come here, I say, but things will be different then. Nobody'll push you around. Not when you've got an older brother who'll smash them if they do.

He laughs but he's got goose bumps so I cover him so he won't get cold and he kicks hard and keeps saying, Yo, Yo for me to lift him up. It's all a game to him and I like to watch him play.

I head back home but when I reach the top of our street where there's a long hill going down I get this funny feeling in my stomach and start pushing the carriage ahead and letting go of it so I have to run to catch up to it. I keep letting it go for longer and longer periods of time and have to run faster and faster to catch it each time. And I'm watching my brother's face. He's squealing with laughter, arms flapping, pounding on the blankets. All a game to him.

And then half-way down, the carriage gets away on me. It rolls in front of me just a few feet and I'm running for all I'm worth but I can't reach it and finally it hits a garbage can and swerves out onto the road. And there's a car coming along. I keep running and hear myself yelling. Part of me is scared for my brother but the biggest part is scared my mother will see.

The car turns to try and miss it and hits the carriage with its side, almost knocking it over but it bounces off and ends up hitting the curb where it stops.

The driver is yelling at me. I say I'm sorry but my back

is to him looking in the carriage at my brother. He isn't laughing or even smiling. His face is serious but his arms are reaching up and he's saying, YO, YO!

I pick him up and he doesn't cry but he holds me tight and trembles a bit like he was cold.

After a week I stopped worrying about my mother finding out.

I'm almost thirteen now and it's nearly winter. My brother is no longer in the backyard when I come home from school. I see much less of him now.

I've had a bad cold for a few days. Sometimes I feel dizzy. I cough a lot and wonder if it's because I've begun to smoke. I have to chew gum so my mother doesn't smell it on my breath. I'm sure she suspects though. She found some matches in my jacket pocket and asked about them. I told her some lie.

Al notices my cough and gives me a bottle of something. Fifteen minutes after the first mouthful I begin to feel better. Not my body but my mind.

Codeine, he warned me when he gave me the stuff. Be careful.

I deliver the rest of the night sipping on the stuff. By the time I go home it's half gone and I'm feeling wonderful. I go home, tell my mother I'm sick and she gives me two aspirins and sends me to bed, which makes me giggle to myself.

I cover myself up warm and begin to drink the rest of the bottle. It feels good. My arms start flapping around on their own and I feel myself bouncing up and down on the bed like I was . . . like I was a baby. The blankets fall off and I don't care. I don't care about anything.

I feel my heart pounding and it's like beautiful drum music. I find I can't move. My muscles are relaxed and I'm going to have a beautiful sleep.

Suddenly my mother is there with a cold, wet cloth on my head and she's patting me and saying, it's okay, the doctor's coming. And I notice I'm vomiting into a pan and my stomach feels torn out and caught in my throat.

I lie there helpless. When I try to move I get dizzy and feel sick again. The doctor is putting something down my throat. And I'm crying.

"Now, now," the doctor says, "I know it hurts but it'll soon be better."

They don't know it but I'm thinking of my brother.

It's the fourth day. Monday. The day to go forth. Yesterday, Sunday, I didn't fool around. There was no excuses. A glass of whisky sat beside my plate at breakfast.

"Gonna be a big day, eh?" Bernice said.

"Yeah, big day."

There had been dreams in the night. Nothing was clear in them. The images were like black-and-white photographs that have been over- or under-exposed. Too much whiteness. Too much blackness. It was like a sign.

"The kids are being picked up for Sunday school," Bernice said. "I'm going over to Mrs. Ferguson's. 'Member she was our landlady when we were over on Clinton. It was her and Al that drove me up to see you. I'm sure they'd like to see you. Why don'tcha come?"

"Not today," I said.

Sunday was the biggest visiting day in prison. It always reminded me of a wiener roast with people from the outside showing up and the conversations and discussions between us became like blazing fires. In due time they brought out their long sticks and skewered us. We melted like marshmallows in the heat.

It didn't seem right that I should be visiting someone my first Sunday out. Especially someone who had visited me.

"They'd really like to see you," she said again.

"I'm not up to it," I said.

"Is that juice?" Lucy asked, pointing at my glass.

"Yes. Vitamins. A tonic for the old man."

"It smells awful," she said, poking her nose in it.

"It's terrible stuff," I agreed.

"I wish you'd come," Bernice persisted.

"Another time. I promise."

"Are you just going to drink?"

"Nope, today's the day I sit down and plan things out. You'll come home to my five-year plan. I'm even going to write it down. You'll have evidence."

She smiled a bit and Cathy looked up expectantly.

"That's fine," Bernice said, "just make sure the ink in that glass doesn't get ahead of you."

She really is a lot tougher now.

"That's not ink," Lucy said. "Daddy said it's tonic."

"I'm only kidding," Bernice said, and it felt like she was. Everything felt looser.

The Sunday school bus arrived and the kids took off on the run. Bernice left shortly after. She kissed me quickly, lightly, like we hadn't been apart for a long time. I liked that.

"I won't be long," she said. "An hour or so."

"Sure. Okay," but my mind was already gone.

I took my drink to the living-room. The facts, I thought. That's what I have to establish.

I'm 29 years old. Have an average intelligence, which means a lot of the time I think too much. I have a reasonable education. High-school diploma. I have a trade that is unusual enough that I never have to worry about getting a job. I have a family. A wife who is considered attractive and even beautiful by some. She is approximately 35 but looks much younger. I have two children, Lucy five and Cathy eleven. On the basis of these facts I must base my future. But I also have a history.

This is the hinge in the creaky door that opens and closes at its own whim. Like a door with no door-jamb that swings to and fro, including and excluding. I have no control over history and no place for it to rest easily.

And suddenly I remember the bank. I'm 23 years old and my life is good, it's very, very good. I'm told that over and over again. I've become a great pantomine and no-one asks how love sits with me. They joke about how obvious it is. My fine job and lovely wife who smiles prettily. My two pretty children. I must be a happy man. And I smiled and nodded because I was trying to learn to believe in something. And like the poem I read somewhere I had learned to dance so well I had become the dance.

The bank robbery happened because my best friend Lenny had a birthday. I'd met him in the reformatory. We hadn't really hung around together but we got out the same day and on the train decided to live together. It'd be cheaper. We

84

became friends. He was best man at my wedding. Later he got married. Our families visited back and forth. He had a good job too. A lovely wife and a new pretty daughter. We kept in touch.

The night he turned 30 we were sitting in a bar. It was August, the same month as my brother's birthday. He could have been my older brother.

"I've had it with this workin' for somebody else," he said. "I sweat my ass off all day while the boss sits in the office and drinks. And what do I get out of it? Nothin'. I've got nothin' to show for it. Even with Carol working we've got nothing but a lot of payments to make. If I could just get my hands on some real money, enough to buy my own place, even enough to rent a spot until I got the business going. In six months I'd be away, Joe."

"Yeah, well look at me," I said. "I make $150 a week. Right?"

"Okay."

"So then I make a little on commission, another $50 say. Right?"

"Yeah."

"And then I steal a little too. $50 or so. I don't know. The thing is I'm still always broke. And then Bernice comes along and you know what she says?"

I remembered he laughed. "You drink too much."

"I don't know how to budget, she says. Shit! I mean what's the use of living if you can't have a good time and spend a few bucks. But there's never enough," I said. And it was true. In those days I worked from nine in the morning till nine at night. On Saturdays I showed up for half a day. When Bernice complained I said I enjoyed my work. In a way I guess I did. I liked talking to the people who came in with their broken cameras and I got a thrill out of having them sit beside me and watch as I repaired. It helped the numbness that was creeping in.

I've never been an athlete but there have been times when I've walked for miles and miles until my body ached. When I was younger I'd often swim out too far from shore and

85

with my body bunched up with fear found the force to make it back where I'd lie in the sand, exhausted and feeling the sweet pain of being alive.

At 23 I was getting numb and after work I'd roam the bars searching for the word that would trigger my fist into a stranger's face, or my body into a woman's arms. Even the hangovers in the morning were welcome diversions. But it was an expensive way to live.

"We should rob a bank," Lenny said.

I've always had great respect for birthdays, so I agreed.

A week later I was in the hospital. Funny, I'd been complaining to Bernice for a long time about my legs, how stiff they were all the time and how easily they swelled up. Her saying, Go to the doctor seemed to make a joke out of it and I'd push it out of my mind. I didn't believe in doctors.

We were going shopping. I'd had a couple of drinks and was feeling fine. All of a sudden though I got dizzy. The wheel in my hand became slippery and I fainted.

I woke up in the emergency ward with a doctor playing on my chest with his stethoscope.

"You trying to kill yourself?" he said.

That's why I didn't like doctors, they speak in such generalities.

"Not that I remember," I said.

"How much have you had to drink today?"

"A couple of shots."

"Have you eaten?"

"I dunno." It was my habit to eat when I was hungry. The pain growling in your gut.

"You know about your heart?" he said.

"Sure."

"You smoke too, eh?"

"A bit."

"Well, this may not mean much to you, but your body was all worked up to have a heart-attack. You know what that is?"

"A heart-attack! Shit, I'm only 23."

Bernice burst through the door carrying Lucy. Cathy

followed slowly behind, her eyes watchful. Bernice was crying.

"Everything's fine," I said. "Too much sun." I tried to swing myself out of the high bed but I felt dizzy again and weak.

"Your husband is going to be with us a couple of weeks," the doctor said.

Lenny came to see me a few days later. He brought a bottle of rye and we sneaked drinks when the nurse went out of the room

"They want to do an operation," I said.

"How come?"

"Well, there's this valve that leaks and screws up the rest of the plumbing. I've had it all my life. It just gives me a pain sometimes, that's all."

"So when are they gonna do it?"

"They're not. I'm getting outa here. The clown who cuts you came to see me and said that seven out of ten of the operations work out perfectly. With the other three, he said there were complications. You know what that means? You're fuckin' dead!"

"Yeah, but. . . ."

"Screw 'em, Lenny, I'm not going this way. I wanted to talk to you about that bank."

Even without the hospital I probably would have decided that way anyway. It was like there were two of me, the Joe Cross people were always congratulating for his great success in life and the real me inside growing smaller and smaller. Like in a way I'd been turned inside out so that all the stuff I said I wanted, like the job with money, the big car, the new house, beautiful Bernice and the kids, had been granted to me as if I'd been blessed with magic wishes. It didn't feel right though. It made me numb. And inside me the real Joe Cross who'd had the dreams in the first place was dying.

Maybe I wasn't ready to grow up.

Ten days later I signed a paper saying I wouldn't hold the

hospital responsible for anything that happened to me. I felt great. Refreshed and rested. And a new plan.

Lenny and I met after work every night and drove around looking for a suitable bank to rob. What seemed most important was one that had the easiest escape route. They all had money, I figured, and getting it wouldn't be too difficult. It was getting away from the place that was tricky. All the downtown banks were eliminated because traffic is too heavy and something like the subway or cabs can't be relied on.

Neither of us had any experience with robbery before but it's strange how much information we discovered we had. Lenny knew we'd have to have two cars. We rented a garage and one night drove to an Eaton's parking lot where we stole a new Chev by running a wire from the distributor across the battery to the starter. We would use this car for the initial getaway and then two or three blocks later switch to our own clean car.

"How much you figger?" Lenny asked.

"Well, if we get a bank with say five tellers, figure about $2000 each and then if I get lucky and the people are cool I might get the floater too. I'm pretty sure the accountant and the head cashier have the key for that and maybe the other cashiers too. Anyway that's good from anywhere to ten to 50 grand."

"Christ!"

We'd decided I'd go in the bank. I wanted to do that and besides Lenny was a better driver.

"Have you told Bernice?" he asked me one day.

"I told Carol. You know, just in case."

Just in case what? It was all a dream.

At last we located the perfect bank. It had an alley in the back where Lenny would wait in the car. I would walk in the front door of the bank, do my business and leave by the side entrance, which was ten feet from the alley. Even out of condition I could run that far. An added bonus we discovered was that the nearest police station that would answer the call would send patrol cars from the east. Our getaway was planned to take us west. By the time the cops stopped to get the details we'd be long gone.

We needed guns, I thought.

"What's happened with you all of a sudden?" Bernice asked me. We were watching TV and necking like we had when I was a kid.

"In love," I said.

"Oh Joe, we're so lucky, aren't we?"

"We sure are," I said.

The kids were in bed. It was still early and we each had a glass of mazeltov with an ice-cube in it. Her favourite wine. I always thought it was too sweet.

"I mean after all we've both been through, to end up like this. Happy together."

"I guess we're just lucky," I said.

Lenny knew a guy who was a second-world-war veteran who had brought back a bunch of hand-guns from Europe. They weren't registered so he couldn't complain or report it if we stole them.

We were lucky. He was on holidays and his house was isolated, so we didn't worry about neighbours while we were breaking in.

We took two guns. Both 32s. One was from Belgium and the other from Germany. They were ugly looking things and I think they made both of us nervous. But we were proud of them.

The bullets were easy to buy.

The night before the robbery I met Lenny and Carol walking on the boardwalk past Cherry Beach. It was a coincidence and it made me feel our lives were special, apart from others. We really were lucky.

"Joe, you're lookin' good," Carol said.

"Worrying always agreed with me," I said.

"You guys be careful tomorrow," she said.

We had an ice-cream cone and watched it get dark. Lenny hardly said anything except when I went to leave.

"I'm not takin' the gun with me tomorrow, Joe."

"Sure," I said. "You won't need it anyway."

Bernice and I watched the late show. She made popcorn with lots of salt and butter, just the way I like it. She was having her period so we didn't make love.

Our plan was for both of us to go to work. We each had an hour for lunch and could easily slip away a few minutes early. We met at the rented garage where Lenny already had the stolen Chev started. I followed him in my car to within three blocks of the bank. I parked and got in with him. I checked the gun under my belt and made sure the note written on a blank cheque was still inside the large camera bag I planned to carry the money in. Everything was set and we'd arrived.

"I'll just be around the back," Lenny said. "Don't be too long."

It was funny, the way he said that. It reminded me of all the times I'd run into the liquor store to get us a bottle while he'd waited, double-parked.

I was wearing a brown suit. It was quite new and tailor-made, so it fit nicely. My hair had been cut recently and I had shaved that morning. I looked neat. I walked into the bank pushing that thought out in front of me. I looked neat and that's how I was going to act. The whole thing was going to be handled neatly.

I was terrified. My body was so tense I thought if I let go it would instantly grow six inches.

I stood in line and waited my turn. Someone lined up behind me.

Bernice had been sleeping when I left that morning. I always made my own breakfast and Cathy had a glass of orange juice with me.

"Will you be home early?" she asked.

"Maybe," I said.

"I'll have somethin' to show you," she said.

The cashier read the note and looked up at me, her mouth smiling and her eyes withdrawn.

"Is this a joke?" she said.

"No joke, and tell the girl next to you to do the same. Just empty your drawer, push it out."

She pushed her own money out but said nothing to the girls next to her. No-one seemed to be noticing anything. Someone behind me waited impatiently, I could hear them shuffling from one foot to the other.

"Okay," I said. "Now I want you to walk back slowly to where the vault is. . . ."

My mouth was so dry I could hardly speak and I was frightened to clear my throat. If I could only swallow everything would be all right.

". . . take all the money you can carry from the floater and bring it back to me. Do it slowly and remember I've got a gun. Don't do anything stupid and no-one gets hurt. I'll be watching you." My voice was soft and, I hoped, calm. The counter was stained from the sweat of my hands. Behind me the feet shuffled.

She didn't move, her terrified eyes locked into mine.

"Would you hurry that, Miss," I said in a louder voice.

Behind me another voice, ". . . slower than the Second Coming."

She began to move, slowly at first and then when she was outside her cage she broke into a jerky run and began to scream.

Holy shit!

"It's a holdup! That man's taking the money!"

Everyone was turning around and looking in different directions. I moved quickly toward the side door. I heard her voice. . . .

"That's him! That's him!"

And out of the corner of my eye I saw someone moving at me. A young guy. Probably the accountant. He heaved himself right over the counter. A fucking athlete. I ran and made the door before him. Round the corner to the alley. Only a few more feet to safety. And then I saw the truck. It had the whole lane blocked.

The gun. The goddamn gun. I got it out just before the guy jumped. I fired once and he was on the ground screaming. At least he wasn't dead, I kept thinking as I headed back toward the corner. Hands reached out to grab me. I kicked someone and heard them swear. I turned the corner and ran the length of the whole block and turned again. The car was there and Lenny put it in reverse.

And then I was falling. My arms gripped tightly around the camera bag with the money so there was nothing to break my fall. A huge man was booting me in the stomach and I couldn't move my hand to get the gun in his direction.

And then Lenny was there, pulling at me while the man continued to kick. I saw Lenny's arm arc and his fist land in the man's groin. He stopped kicking me and Lenny lifted me to the car.

He raced away and his voice was screeching more than the tires.

"What happened! For Christ's sake Joe, what didya do?"

I was hurting but in a way fast becoming numb too. For me it was over. Lenny had to worry about the driving.

"A little trouble," I said.

"I heard a shot. Didya have to shoot?"

"Just once Lenny, don't worry. Just get us to the other car."

"No time," he said. "No time for that. We'll be okay with this."

"Lenny, we gotta change. 50 people got this number!"

"No, no, we're okay. We just gotta be cool."

His face was drenched with sweat and he was driving 60. We flashed through a red light.

"Lenny!" I screamed, "we're gonna get caught like this."

He said nothing, concentrating on the driving and then I saw a dark blue car pass us, stop and make a U-turn.

"Cops," I said.

We were on St. Clair Avenue now. Lenny darted up side-streets taking corners on two wheels. The car twisted and bumped across curbs. I sat there looking in the camera bag at the money and the gun in my lap. I wasn't scared anymore. Lenny would get us out of it. I wondered if I should shoot at the cop. I didn't want to.

At Spadina the car skidded across the intersection and

bounced up on a lawn. Lenny opened the door and jumped out.

"Com'on!"

I was surprised. Didn't he know I couldn't run? I was too tired. But I wasn't just going to sit there either. Fuck 'em all.

The car was still running and I slid over behind the wheel. The cop had stopped and was walking toward the car with his gun out. He was still a long distance away though and I roared the motor and took off.

It was a good straightaway on Spadina south of St. Clair. I had the thing flat out and the speedometer needle dipped back and forth around the hundred mark. There was a corner ahead, a flashing red warning light. A sign saying to slow to fifteen. All I had to do was make that and I was away.

I tried to gear down a bit. The car was an automatic. Nothing happened. I touched the brakes lightly and the car began to skid. I pushed harder and jerked the wheel around. It wobbled for a second and the next instant I was crashing into the stone wall of Casa Loma, one of Toronto's big tourist attractions.

It seemed to take a long time for the noise of breaking things to stop. And then it was so quiet I thought I was dead. What a relief, I thought. Now it's all over.

Later I managed to pull my head back through the windshield and get my chest unstuck from the steering-wheel. I remember I was laughing and it felt like I had the hiccoughs.

When the cop shot me I think I was trying to light a cigarette.

The ambulance came and I felt relaxed even when I heard from far away someone say, "This fucker's had it."

Bernice had a priest waiting at the hospital and I was given the last rites even though I'd never been in a Catholic church.

They had to remove three ribs, they were so badly smashed. My sternum was broken. I might be blind in one eye if I lived, they said. And they weren't sure how bad the concussion was.

But it only took six weeks to get me back together again. A policeman sat in my room at the hospital and Bernice visited me with the kids. She wasn't allowed to bring anything. Not even cigarettes. The policeman had to buy them for me.

They caught Lenny running through Winston Churchill Park. He pleaded guilty the first day in court and was sentenced to four years.

Seven weeks later I appeared, not fully recovered but certainly rested and refreshed. The judge didn't feel I took the proceedings seriously enough.

He remarked several times that I should wipe the smirk off my face. I wasn't allowed to talk or I would have explained it was a scar left from the accident.

Bernice wailed on the witness stand, testifying to what a good husband I was, that she and the children needed me.

"That is my only consideration in this case," he said. "The fact that you have such a fine family willing to stand behind you, an employer willing to speak up for you. Obviously you are an intelligent man and only need to learn a lesson so you may return and take your place in society again. Therefore against my desire to be harsh I sentence you to twelve years in the penitentiary."

Shit, I thought, at the very worst I'd only be 35 when I got out. And in the meantime I was safe.

That's how I spent Sunday, remembering that day and wondering again what I meant when I thought of safety. Safety from what?

I trembled thinking about it all over again. It always did that to me. It was more than fear. It was like a head-lock that made my whole body ache but I knew there was a way to get out of it. A certain move or gesture. If only I could remember what it was.

So Sunday again, I drank too much. Bernice returned and I tried to talk. To function. To explain how I was going to make it all up to them. She took the kids out somewhere for the afternoon and everything sort of faded. Like a movie being over and during intermission you're not quite sure what to do with yourself until the next one comes on.

There's no-one to talk to about the one you've just seen or explain things you don't understand.

It's Monday. The fourth day. The day to go forth. Onward Christian soldiers, marching as to war. . . . Living is like that. An undeclared war, and marching, always marching. If I were a man I would identify the enemy. I would pursue him and end his life.

"Daddy, breakfast's ready," Cathy says.

The balcony is my kingdom.

"Coming."

I'm sitting at the table with them, unwashed and smelly; the traveller who travels only the high road.

"Your father looks quite fine this morning," Bernice says.

"He looks awful to me," Lucy says.

They ignore me.

A career. I need a career. Obviously this one is not my piece of cake. I'm not cut out for it. So, something completely new. A vision of myself set loose in the woods with a fly-swatter, a killer of bugs, black flies, mosquitoes, all species of irritating insects. Just me and the birds and the frogs and toads who eat them too. Crushing buzzing skulls from morning till night. Billions of them. Trillions. A service to mankind. But in the end someone would write a tale of my exploits and raise the final question: how to separate the bugs from the killer of bugs.

"Are you going for that job interview?" Bernice asks.

"Yes, right after the three esses, shave, shower, you know."

"You're feeling pretty good for someone who drank everything in sight and then passed out."

I'm not going to be public with my feelings. It's bad enough living with them inside.

"My youthful spirit," I say.

"We're going swimming," Lucy says. "You wanna come with us, Daddy?"

"Love to, but I gotta get a job today. Maybe when I get back I'll meet you at the pool."

"Oh boy, Daddy's gonna come swimmin' with us!"

95

"If he gets back in time," Cathy says. Already I see money coming out of every pay cheque to start a fund for her to go to law school.

They're getting ready to leave. The day is moving.

"Don't forget towels," Bernice says.

Lucy almost knocks over my cup of coffee jumping in my lap.

"Gimme a kiss, eh Daddy?"

I hold her for a second, my hands still not sure of her shape.

At the door Cathy turns to me. "Good luck," she says.

We're alone. My betrothed and I. Together in the same trough.

"You must feel awful," she says. "Maybe you could call him and get the appointment changed."

"No, really, I'm fine."

She pours herself a cup of coffee and sits down. This woman out of the thousands, millions, perhaps even billions, who is my wife. Her hair long and dark, dark and her eyes when she looks at me, darker.

"What's gonna happen to us, Joe?"

"We'll be okay."

"It's still the same for you, isn't it?" she says.

"What?"

"I don't know. Whatever it is inside of you. I never knew what it was and thought after all this time it would've gone away. But it's no different."

"Nothing's the same, Bernice. I mean we're older and different things have happened to us. Things that neither of us know about for the other person. There are things I don't know about you anymore."

"But why do you always have to know?"

"I dunno."

It's true. I don't.

"You don't trust anybody, Joe. Not even yourself."

"I try."

"You try. You try! Big deal. You know, when you were in prison I found out one day that I wasn't any more lonely than when you were home. That made me scared, Joe. Do you ever get lonely?"

"Look, I've got to get going or I'm gonna be late."

"Scared to admit the truth?"

"No, Bernice, but I don't see any point to this. We'll be okay. Right now I'm worried about that job."

And then she's crying.

"I'm sorry," she says. "Joe, I'm really sorry. I just don't want it to be the way it used to be."

The way it used to be. Was it so bad? I'm trying hard to remember the way it used to be so I can make it that way again. I thought some of it was pretty good.

"Everything's going to be okay," I say. I'm like a pilot with the plane's engines all gone who keeps telling the passengers over and over again: everything's fine, ladies and gentlemen, just remain seated.

I clean myself up and get dressed. An old brown suit still fits me. I look in the mirror and see a serious man staring back at me, his eyes a little bloodshot.

Bernice kisses me at the door.

"Good luck, Joe."

With all the luck I'm lugging around I feel I should be going to a poker game.

The bus gives me the creeps. People staring at me, their eyes like suns, my body getting softer, melting. I hold tightly to the strap, afraid of floating away. I'm an unacknowledged astronaut suspended from a hook in a chugging bus. If I lose my grip I'll be lost.

The president of the company is introducing me to the new manager of the service department.

"This is Joseph Cross," he says.

"Yes, yes," the worried man named Frank says. He's heard of me.

"Some of the fellows have mentioned you," he says.

He shows me around the service area, which is bigger now. There are new machines that I don't recognize. People who remember me shake my hand.

"Comin' back to work, Joe?" one of them asks.

"Hope so."

And then the three of us are in the manager's office politely drinking coffee.

"So you're free and available," the president says. I remember when he was sales-manager. The promotion hasn't shaken his confidence.

"Yeah, I'd really like to get back working as soon as I can."

"How long's it been, Joe, four, almost five years now, isn't it?"

"It's been a while."

"Things have changed a lot in that time," Frank, the service-manager says.

"Yes, there have been some remarkable advances made," the president says.

"I figured I'd have to go through a kind of retraining period," I say. "While I was away though I had all the trade magazines sent to me so I managed to keep up with the ideas. It's just the experience of the practical work that I need."

"Trouble is," Frank says, his fingers in his mouth, "trouble is, there's people on the assembly line who've had their names in for the service department for months. We can only train one person at a time and it's usually easier with someone who's been on the line because at least they're familiar with the product. We've got one person training now, see. . . ."

"Is that right?" the president says. "I didn't know that."

I'm feeling very panicky. There's a voice saying, well, you made a try at it. They don't want you or need you. So get out. I'd really like to leave. The coffee is making me sick and I'm trying hard not to gag.

"When I worked here before there was always a backlog of old cameras that needed repairing but nobody liked doing them because parts were hard to find. Do you still have that?"

"We still get old cameras," Frank admits. He's wearing

98

a white coat like a doctor and his desk is scattered with papers. I know without asking that he doesn't do any repairing himself.

"Why don't you hire me to fix those?" I say.

"There wouldn't be enough to keep you going," he says.

"How many have you got?"

"Oh, I don't know. A few."

The bastard! I saw a whole wall of shelves that were full of them. Enough work for a year.

"See, while I was fixing the old ones I could keep my eyes open and in my spare time learn about the new models. I pick things up fast."

I shouldn't have said that. The guy's beginning to sweat, scared I'll do him out of his job.

"I don't know," he says. "I'm still concerned with the assembly-line people."

"Tell you what, Joe," the president says. "Give us a few days to think about it. Frank and I'll discuss it and see if something can't be worked out. Then I'll give you a call. Okay, Joe?"

"Sure, that's great. I appreciate it."

He's not a bad guy and he's honest enough to call me and tell me no to my ear.

"The other thing," Frank says as I get up to leave, "all our employees have to be bonded. I only mention it because I figure it might present some difficulty for you."

He must be getting pretty desperate. Maybe there's a chance for me after all.

"I'd forgotten about that too," the president says.

"It's no problem. The parole people will arrange all that."

"Fine," they both say, one more distinctly than the other. They're shaking my hand and I'm leaving. They don't wish me good luck.

I'm on the bus again.

I register at the employment office. A man gives me a number with a card on it. He says there are no jobs in my line and he wishes me luck.

On the bus I have a strange feeling of responsibility. I

have a sense that I could cry easily but the feeling is some-thing like the first glow of being high too. All the energy in me is under control. I can handle anything.

I no longer have to hold a strap in the bus. It's later in the day and there are fewer people, so I have a seat. Maybe that's changed things. I could always see more clearly sitting down.

I go to the welfare office and fill out a form. I wait and then a woman calls me.

"What's a young fellow like you doing here?" she says.

It sounds like a variation on a bad joke. I could ask her the same about herself.

"Outa work," I say. "The people at the employment office have nothing for me. I've got a family."

"How long have you been out of work?" her pencil poised.

"Almost five years."

"Oh?"

"I was in prison. I just got out Friday."

"Oh."

She takes the name of my parole officer and tells me someone will come to the house to visit us. Tomorrow someone will come to investigate. I should be at home. After the visit a report will be made and I'll get a cheque.

I leave and I'm on the bus again. I head for home. I feel satisfied with my efforts. Things aren't so bad.

Bernice is washing the dishes. She's also singing. I can't remember ever hearing her sing before. I think of a young deer discovered drinking at a mountain pool. Her slender arms moving back and forth in the dishwater, her back slightly arched. She catches my scent and all motion and sound is suspended. She turns quickly and her voice is startled, unwilling it seems to let go of the song.

"Joe!"

"I'm back."

"How'd it go?"

I review my day for her. She looks relaxed. At home.

"You think they'll call?" she asks.

"I think so. He's pretty good about things like that."

"So now we wait."

"For a day or so. I'll phone some other places too."

"How are you feeling?"

"Better. Is there anything left around to drink? A beer?"

"I think there's a couple of beers."

"That's what I need. I'm so goddam dry."

"Shall I cook you some lunch?"

"No, I'm gonna go over and meet the kids."

I think I should ask her to come with me but the thought has come too late. When I think of Bernice, too often I think of my duty. Times like today I feel good having done what I know I should. Being responsible. Is that how it is between people, doing the right thing and being rewarded like a dog with little pats on the head? Only with Cathy does it feel different. I do things for her because I have to. I have to for myself.

There's this cold thing between Bernice and me today. I've done the right thing but she isn't sure of me. I could have spent the whole morning in the park. I have no proof of my good intentions. There's no real way to make up for what I am except maybe to change.

If I were a magician I'd hide in my magic hat and wait for the world to pull out the rabbit when they needed it.

I sip at the cold beer and feel the urge build slowly in me to do something. And I think of my mother.

I go into the other room and dial the number.

She doesn't seemed surprised.

"Did your wife tell you your brother helped her move?"

She doesn't believe in Bernice as a real living person with a name.

"No, she never mentioned it."

"I sent him over just a couple of months ago too with a bunch of stuff I thought she could use."

The junk cleared out after spring house cleaning.

"I'm sure she really appreciated it. How are you?"

"Good. I'm fine. Never a sick day in my life. You know.

Just when I had your brother, that was the only time. How long. . . ."

"Just since Friday, so I'm still getting settled."

"What're you going to do?"

"Get a job. You know."

"You're gonna stay living there then?"

"Sure."

"I thought after all that time."

"Nothing changes that much, Mom."

"It does, Joe. Your father's going blind. Cataracts on both eyes. Just like his mother."

"I wrote him a letter. It was kind of a crazy thing. Did he tell you about it?"

"Never mentioned it, but that's not unusual. I mean, when did he ever tell me anything?"

"It was a crazy letter, like I say. I was trying to get to know him. I always felt bad because I never got to know him. So I tried to explain that."

"He's a closed book," she says.

"Is he still working?"

"Sure. Up every morning at seven, same as always, gets his own breakfast now though. I don't see any need for me to get up now that Dan's not here."

"You'd think he'd be tired of the business."

"It's his whole life. That and golf, except now he can't see to play too well. He says he's trying to sell it and then he'll have the operation but I don't have much faith in that. I think he was really hurt when he found out Dan wasn't going to take it over."

"Yeah, I guess he would be. He worked so hard to build it up."

"But it was stupid for him to ever think of Dan doing that, a job where you never get your hands clean. I told him ten years ago when he had the name changed to Fair and Son that it was all a pipe-dream. So now he's 67 and he'll probably keep plodding along in the place day after day until he can't see a thing or he drops dead."

So that's how it ends, always in the dark.

"I'd like to talk to him sometime."

"There's not many left for him to talk to. Harry, his best friend, 'member he used to golf with him all the time?"

"Yes."

"Well, he's dead. Had a stroke. Some of the others too. I mean there was never very many anyway. Always kept to himself, so now he works late nights like he used to and I hardly ever see him."

"It's a bad way to end your life," I say. There's a sadness in me for not knowing this man. The sadness is mine, different from hers, something not easily explained or shared.

"But you know," she says. "I've learned something from him. Yeah, I really have. I used to sit around waiting. All the time waiting and hoping our lives would change, that we'd have good times. You know me. I mean I'm no old woman, there's twelve years between us. So one day I just made up my mind to do things and now I've got to admit I'm pretty happy. . . ."

And then she began to cry.

"Is it so selfish of me to want to have fun?" she says. "You understand, Joe, you always did what you wanted. Even when you were small you figured out ways to get what you wanted."

That's the way it looked, I suppose. I never really thought about it before.

"So now I'm on the Ladies' Auxiliary at the church and I help with the dances they have every second Friday. It's mostly people my age who come. Not really old but, you know. And I dance and I have a good time. Sometimes one of the bachelors drives me home, we've got quite a few and I don't care, I enjoy it when they flirt with me."

The spirit is back in her voice. It speaks of a pride I've never heard before.

"You say you got this from the old man. I still don't understand."

"Don'tcha see?" she says. "He's made a choice. I mean, he lives the way he does because he wants to. So I decided for myself too. Do you think that's wrong, Joe?"

"No, I think everybody should do that if they can."

"I thought you would, Joe. Oh it's so nice to talk to you again. We always understood each other. Why don't you phone me next week and we'll arrange to have lunch? I'd just love to sit down with you and talk, Joe. Will you call me?"

"Sure I will."

"Good, I'll look forward to your call. It's so nice to hear from you again and this time I'm sure things are going to be better for you."

"Thanks," I say. "I'll call."

"Bye then," she says.

"Bye."

Bernice is watching me. She's been in the room a long time now, standing across from me and waiting for me to finish.

"Your mother?" she says.

"Yeah,"

"Did she ask about the kids."

"No."

"She never does."

"She forgets, Bernice, that's all."

"She never calls me by my name."

I'm thinking of my old man, about the kind of choices he has made and wondering if he did make them. Maybe my mother is just claim-jumping. Maybe the promised land my mother thinks he travels in is just the territory he has accepted as his allotted space and from where she sits the grass looks greener. He's built fences though as if he meant to stay there. His whole life fenced in and now she calls it ownership and perhaps it's only protection.

"What're you thinking about?" Bernice asks. "You've got that faraway look."

"My old man."

"Is he sick?"

"Sort of, but mostly he's just old. I don't know him. It makes me wonder about myself and how the kids must feel about me."

"They love you," she says.

"But they don't know me."

"What does that mean even?"

"I suppose you're right. I just don't want to die that lonely."

Her arms come round me. I'm pulled beyond my own senses, past my own fences and her body lying on the couch opens to me like a gate. I enter a kingdom that is not of my own making. With her hands forcing me closer I think of a God who has made this moment in his mind and for some secret reason has shared it with us.

Her hips lift me and lower me gently. I'm being rocked into my sweetest dream.

"That was lovely, lovely," I say.

"For me too," she says, but I know that already. It makes me think of the difficulty of saying I love you to another person. The difficulty I have. The words get said when they are needed only. When there is love the words are almost comic and you can laugh at them.

"I love you, Joe Cross," she says, and yes, she's laughing.

"Me too," I say, and she laughs louder and tickles me.

But now I want to leave. Times like this are rare and to linger over them, to try and prolong them, is dangerous. It's too easy to hurt or be hurt at such times and the biggest hurt, the hurt that's always there, when your bodies cool and withdraw from each other, this is the only hurt that you should remember. The honest hurt.

I get up and dress slowly. I feel weak, perhaps I'm hungry. She lies watching me, following my movements so I feel I'm dancing.

"It's after two," I say. "I'm gonna go meet the kids."

"Were you afraid today?" she asks.

I think about that.

"I was nervous. After a while though I remembered things and I was more calm."

"I was proud that you went. I would've been scared to face all those people. Especially when they all know."

"It wasn't so bad and I feel better that I did it. Even if I don't get the job there I know now that things will work out for me."

"Yes," she says. "I felt that when you came back. It was like the old Joe. You marched in like a king."

"You were singing."

"I heard you though."

"My queen."

I kiss her mouth and leave her lying there naked, her face smiling and her eyes misted with a fog like a pair of lakes on an early summer morning.

The sun is hot. It's a day I suppose like many other days. I've felt this heat before but today there's a new burning sensation. It's a slightly scary feeling like enjoying the warmth of a fire and heaping more and more logs on it so the flames climb higher and extend further, but knowing the supply of fuel is limited. Tomorrow it could be cold and there would be no wood left to burn.

I'm walking through the park toward the pool and around me people are moving. Some of them are in groups doing things together. Others are alone and like me, walking. A few are lying on the grass. I don't see anyone running by himself, only the occasional child propelled by some inner wind. The groups of people remind me of fat knots or a lassoo that's become tangled and tries to regain its shape by twisting and turning. The people are like stiffened pieces of rope used by magicians to do climbing tricks. We are all slightly mechanical in our movements, so sure of what we're doing and not thinking about it, we've forgotten. We are props in a play who know the script better than the actors. We are all being phased out. Dying.

The people by themselves don't have any toys. One old man who is walking slowly has a cane, but this doesn't seem to qualify. The others have baseballs and bats, beach-balls are being bounced from person to person and frisbies are being tossed back and forth between people, their movements dependent on it and on each other. A relationship of convenience perhaps.

The time passes for us all in various ways.

Most of the children seem to have a vehicle of some kind. There are red-and-yellow tricycles, silver-and-gold flashing racing bikes and even the babies are being pushed in carriages and strollers. But at some point in life we all must stand on our own feet. Perhaps ballet dancers are the only ones who understand the fine balance of being taller middle-stage in a glaring light. Most of us tip-toe in the dark, frightened to wake someone.

And in the end we are all carried away.

The trees are heavy with their own growth. I envy them their leaves, the proof it seems to offer of their being alive. Many of the trees have initials carved into them, scars left by people who are defined in the end by lying in wooden boxes with their names above them in stone. Something to remember them by.

In prison my number was 3274. In the year 1974 I will be 32. An end or only a beginning? It's hard not to believe in signs. The leaves begin to fall from the trees, the days grow shorter. The first snow comes. And then the ice. The air is brittle in your lungs. I always feel stronger in the winter. But then when you've become accustomed to it and are sure of your footing, the firmness leaves the earth. The ground becomes soft, unsettled, unwilling to accept itself. But then the sun burns everything hard. Things are frozen again. For a time it is easier to move, until things begin to break. Finally rot.

These are signs we all know and have long ago accepted and forgotten. Now we listen for the tapping sound under the hood of our car to become louder. We make some move to salvage the machinery.

A mother listens to the sound of a cough growing larger in her child's chest. She telephones out. Something is prescribed. Later it's delivered and administered to the unknowing child. The child survives.

Two people, a man, a woman, although not always, embrace less closely than before and the distance between them is like a pointed stick. Their special intimacy impales them and they are wounded, bleed, sometimes real blood. They are reduced to separate corners where they heal and grow mellow in their pain. The scars left are always on the back, usually at the base of the spine. These they can share the sight of but because there's no agreement between them they often stand in rooms back to back and in bed this is now the accepted posture.

Always there are signs of other things to come. These signs change the moment, alter it sometimes beyond repair.

I once saw a man in joy, a friend new with a wife. This love made him do simple things. He bought a canoe to take with them on a holiday. A red canoe to float in, the flood of feelings that threatened sweet death by drowning. She was frightened of the water though and the first day she stood on the shore and waved. He couldn't see this because he had no choice but to paddle away. Afterwards it was always like that with her, sometimes waiting on the shore when he returned. One cold night when he was short of firewood he burned the extra paddle.

The grass is green in this park. There are many voices raised in loud playful noises. It's impossible to hear the silent ones and I'm not sure how many there are. I too am quiet, my voice closed, there being no-one to open it to. Only my feelings are loud, they flutter inside of me like birds.

In the park, the birds are strangely absent from the trees. The skies are empty of them. They may all be dead or sleeping. I have always feared the death happening around me, I fear there will be nothing left living to whom I can give an account of my own.

In the park, the trees are all cedar. There is no room among them for a birch to grow to its proper size.

When I was thirteen I learned about eating soil under your feet. About roots.

My name was Joseph Fair then. My mother let my hair grow long and it was held in place by bobby-pins that were always falling out. The other kids called me hairy-fairy. I didn't mind. I learned early to ignore things.

The earliest thing I remember was being pushed on a swing by an old woman in a black dress. She pushed me higher and higher and my screams got louder and louder until I could no longer hear my fear. Most people have similar memories.

Until I was seven a woman came to my home once a week and drove me to the hospital in her car. In the hospital my name was Joseph Cross. It was like a game and I listened to the doctors who talked behind closed doors about the future death of the Joe named Cross.

He was dying. In a year they whispered. Sooner, later. There was nothing they could do. He must rest. That was the only hope. Sleep, sleep.

I was put to bed every night at six. In the summer I lay in bed and watched the sun dance across the floor. Sometimes I would sit on the edge of the bed with my bare feet dangling in the pool of heat. I had no real brother then to talk to, just a memory or maybe a dream.

By the time I was eight I'd grown stronger, visits to the hospitals were less frequent.

For a time my life became a pact with wood. I touched wood for life. Everything around me was made of wood and just in case I carried a knot of it in my pocket. It was a safe time. I delivered papers, running from my wooden waggon or sled, after first touching its surface, to the customer's milk-box with its wooden door, which I'd touch at least twice, once when arriving and once when leaving. Wood was rarely out of my mind, or my hands.

My mother called me moody, withdrawn and the lady came in the car and at the hospital there were different tests with a different doctor. I still don't know the results.

I can't remember the exact moment I found out. It grew in me, a stirring at first, then a restlessness, finally an awareness that my life was lived in a clearing, a place set apart in a forest, and that all the other trees around me, even those whose branches sometimes touched me, grew on different ground. Higher or lower, wetter or drier, some subtle thing. The rain and sun reached us in different ways.

I asked about my name. I remember it was shortly after

Christmas. The decorations were still up. The wreath on the front door. We never put one on the back.

I asked my mother. It was the middle of the day and my father wasn't home.

"How come in the hospital they always called me a different name? And how come I've got to sign forms like that one in the fall when I wanted to play football and I had to put down Joseph Cross instead of Joe Fair? Is there something going on?"

She sat down right away, her hands searching for a cigarette.

"You see," she said. "We weren't allowed to adopt you. . . ."

"Adopt me?"

"Yes, you see, your mother. . . ."

"My mother, but. . . .?"

"Listen Joe! Just listen! When you were a baby, you were very sick. In those days they didn't have the medicines like they do now. So your mother, the woman you were born to, she was young and there were other children. Your father was away at the war. She got tired of it, I guess. She just left one day. Your grandmother looked after you for a while but she was too old and so she had to put you somewhere where you'd be looked after. You were put in the Children's Aid and after a while they called us because we had our name in to adopt a baby. We'd been told we wouldn't have children of our own. We went to a lot of doctors and they all told us the same, so we put our name in because we wanted to have our own son."

"So you got me."

"Yes, but we weren't allowed to adopt you because you were so sick. They said we wouldn't be able to afford all the medical expenses and later when you got well we could adopt you then."

"But you didn't."

"After so long we never thought about it. We've raised you as our son. You're as much our son as your brother Dan."

"Except he really is your son."

"It's not like that," she said, and her face was twisted, partly angry and partly sad. I guess I felt the same.

The arguments that followed were between my mother and me. My brother was too young to understand what was going on and my father refused to discuss it.

I wanted to leave, to explore whatever it was that was released when I finally learned the truth.

"I don't belong here," I said over and over. "You have no right. . . ."

We hit out at each other with all the weapons available.

"How can you be so ungrateful . . . so callous with our feelings . . . think of all we've done for you . . . loved you . . . taken you into our home . . . raised you like a son."

"You lied to me . . . you should've told me . . . it shows you never trusted me . . . I was always treated different."

The gulf between us was filled with a raging fire, our words fresh fuel that made it burn more hotly and forced us to step back from the edge until we could no longer reach each other.

I threatened to run away. I had before. She knew I would and the battle would be lost, so she ended it abruptly one day by packing my bags while I was at school and phoning the social worker who had always driven me to the hospital. She was waiting to take me when I got home.

I remember it was the day before Valentine's. I had lived eleven years of my thirteen in that house. My mother was preparing supper and she didn't come to the door when we left. After that day I never lived there again.

The park grass is moist under my feet. At night men come here and gather the dew-worms that are then sold as bait to be put on hooks, lowered into the water and snatched at by fish who are then themselves caught.

It's strange and kind of exciting to realize that there is always something living under your life and something under that life, forever it seems.

I wonder if the kids are really waiting for me. For me, I mean.

The swimming-pool is enclosed behind a wire fence. I search among the moving figures for the children. And then I see Cathy sitting at the edge of the pool, her eyes raised and watchful. I look beyond her and see Lucy's small body swaying as she climbs the steps of a slide. She reaches the top and stands poised for a second, her eyes searching the arena below. She locates her sister and raises her arm in a wave. Cathy waves back. Lucy's mouth moves but she's too far away for either of us to hear, and then she launches herself down the slide, her arms flung out, and her body curled up so that she slides mostly on her back and hits the water behind first. The water is very shallow and Lucy emerges quickly, spitting water but smiling. Cathy smiles back and waves.

As Lucy joins the line for the slide I wonder how many times today this performance has been repeated.

There's no line-up to get inside. It's late in the season and a week-day. The only adults around are the life-guards and the odd mother. They give me a box for my clothes and a number to pin to my bathing-suit. The point of the pin nicks my flesh and the blood is very red against my white skin.

Cathy is still sitting at the edge of the pool. Even her feet are out of the water but she's shivering and her thin body is hunched up, her elbows pulled tight together in front of her like closed doors.

"Hi," I say.

Still tightly coiled, she turns. "Hi," she says.

"Where's your towel? You look like you're freezing."

"It got wet. I'm okay though."

She stands up and watches the end of the slide. Lucy appears and waves. She sees me and waves so frantically that she stumbles and falls face first in the water. She pops up quickly but there's fear on her face as she tries to smile and beside me Cathy is even more knotted up, her legs crossed tensely.

"One of these days she's gonna drown herself," she says.

"Do you always watch her like this?"

"She hasn't got any sense so somebody's got to."

Lucy is back in the line. We both watch her quietly for a few minutes, the two-piece blue bathing-suit that threatens to fall off and her long hair, lighter than anybody else's in our family, now wet and dark and hiding her face from us, her small hand constantly in motion to keep it swept back, probably so she can see us.

"How'd it go?" Cathy asks.

"The job?"

"Yeah, did you get it?"

"Dunno. Said they'd phone."

"Can't you tell though?"

"Whaddaya mean?"

"I mean if they, well you know, if they like you."

She loves you, yeah, yeah, yeah. She loves you and you know that can't be bad. She loves you and you know you should be glad.

If they like me.

"I guess I never thought about it," I say. "I mean I just want the job. It doesn't matter if they don't like me. I don't care as long as I get the job."

"If you don't get it, will you have to go back?"

I put my towel around her shoulders and leave my arm there to hold her. She's rigid against me. Above us the sun is hot. I'm reminded of the exercise yard in the prison, there was no place to find shade there either.

"No, that won't happen," I say. "It'd take a long time with me having no job before anything like that could happen."

"Before you did something bad to go there. Could you go back again even if you didn't do something bad?"

"I suppose. It's up to my parole officer. I don't think so though."

"Why did you do it?" she asks.

Lucy is sliding toward the water and we can hear her yell.

"Do what?"

"You know. Whatever it was. Mommy said it was bad."

"I was mixed up," I say. It's hard to explain a need to die.

To get things over with. I was tired of waiting for whatever it was that was going to happen. I was scared.

"And now it's okay?"

"In a way, I guess. I mean I'm home. It's all over."

She turns and looks up at me, her face as unrevealing as a light-bulb. I see her suddenly as a person with secrets. She's grown up without me. It's not a sad thing for the moment but I know there will be times when I'll want to weep for her. Blood is an ephemeral thing and the things that join people have warped between us. We grow at different angles.

"You won't do it again?" she says.

"No."

It's quiet between us for a minute. A white butterfly has made it over the fence but the smell of the chlorine in the water drives it away.

"Yesterday in Sunday school they told us a story," Cathy says. "It was about a man God wanted to do something for him. But the man didn't want to do it, so he ran away.

The trouble is everywhere he ran God followed him and finally the man was on a ship in the ocean and God made a bad storm so it looked like the ship was going to sink. The other men on the ship were scared and they heard God's voice talking to the man he wanted to help him but the man still refused. So later the sailors got mad at the man and threw him overboard and then a whale swallowed him. And he lived inside the whale's stomach a long time until finally he did what God wanted him to do."

"Did you like that story?"

"Not exactly like it. I thought it was mean for God to make the man do something he didn't want to, but it had a happy ending because the man was glad when he did what he was supposed to."

"Sometimes it works out that way. I think mostly in stories though. Lots of times I do things that I'm supposed to and I don't feel so great about it."

"Me neither," she says.

We both laugh.

"Do they tell you lots of stories like that?"

"Yeah, every week, except I don't go every week. Only sometimes, but all the time I do they have a different story or sometimes the same one, like every year at Christmas, about Jesus and the stable and everything."

"My mother used to give me a quarter for collection when I was a little kid and every week I'd go and buy twenty cents worth of candy and only put a nickel on the plate."

She laughs.

"I do that sometimes too." And her face more serious, "Is that a sin?"

"I don't think so. I mean I never heard any story where God asked for money. I remember the story where Jesus threw some guys out of the church because they were making money."

"The money-changers," she says. "I heard that one too."

"No, I don't think God wants your money. To me it's like going to the movies. If you didn't pay the man who runs the place he would have to close up and the people who made the movies and were actors wouldn't be able to do it anymore."

"I like watching TV better," she says and we laugh again.

Lucy climbs the steps of the slide more slowly now. She's getting tired. Cathy is still aware of her but she's less watchful now, more prone to look away. It's me who's tense now, watching the small child labouring to reach the top, older kids behind her pushing and shoving.

She steadies herself at the top, waves and lets go. But before she has reached the bottom and hit the water a boy behind her, a ten- or twelve-year-old boy pushes off and races down behind her. His feet hit the back of her neck just as her feet touch the water. It's a rare thing for me to see something before it's actually happened and I'm in the water and halfway to her before her head disappears. The water is shallow and I pull her up easily. She has swallowed more water than usual. She coughs and chokes on it and I grab the boy, yank him to me and slap him heavily with the back of my hand against his chest.

"Watch it!" I say and he's surprised, not at what he has

done or almost done but that someone else has seen it. He ducks under the water and swims away. I carry Lucy to the side of the pool where Cathy's waiting.

"What happened?" she says. Her face is pinched with worry and guilt like a sentry that has fallen asleep.

"Nothing," I say.

"That boy pushed me," Lucy says, and she points.

"You're okay," I say and help her snuggle under the towel with her sister who is no longer shivering.

"You gonna swim with us?" Lucy asks.

"In a minute, after you get a rest and get warm."

"I'm not cold."

"How come you're shaking then? Is that a new dance?"

"Well, I'm just a little cold."

Cathy's eyes skim the water's surface like the steel blade of a knife. "If I see that guy," she says, "I'll smash him."

"Daddy already hit him," Lucy says.

"Let's forget about it," I say. "He won't do it again."

"Daddy, how come you never made us purses yet?" Lucy asks.

But Cathy is looking at me as if she's surprised about something. And then her face clears and she takes my hand and squeezes it so softly it may not have happened at all.

"I haven't had time," I answer.

"Will you make them soon?"

"Sure."

"I want mine to be red and black," Lucy says.

"I don't care about the colour of mine," Cathy says.

The water at our feet is cloudy blue. I notice the one-piece red bathing suit Cathy wears is too tight and leaves pink welts where it cuts in at the shoulders and thighs. She's growing. Her eyes are brown like Bernice's. Lucy's are blue like mine or like the sky with its white clouds. Her eyes aren't cloudy though. Both their skins are brown. My hand resting on my knee is a shade of orange and the skin of my legs is white under gold hairs. Our separate lives measured in different colours.

"Let's go swimming," I say.

116

"The slide," Lucy yells.

And then we're racing through the cold water, climbing the steps, giggling, laughing, and Cathy sits on my legs and Lucy is tucked in tight behind her against my stomach and we slide down screaming, with me the toboggan.

And then it's time to leave. It's nearly supper time. Changing in separate rooms and waiting outside for them, the sun still hot. And running through the park. Lucy sometimes on my shoulders and for short times Cathy. Going home. In me, a great tiredness, my mind dreaming of sleep.

It's Tuesday. The fifth day. I'm in bed beside my wife. It's early. The sun is waiting in the wings. There's no pain to greet me. I have had a night of natural sleep. And the dreams. Always when I take no precautions the dreams come. In prison they gave me sleeping pills and the drug was like a blanket of sand on my mind, nothing would grow and the climate was comfortable.

Last night they weren't bad dreams, only puzzling. There were no men in my dreams. There was a crowd of women who seemed to grow larger as time passed. A figure who resembled my mother seemed to be leading them in a dance. Certainly there was music but its rhythm escaped me. I tried desperately to remember the tune so I could school my feet and not go stumbling about as each woman in turn took me in her arms. I tried too hard to remember and in the end they formed a circle and began talk to me, each talking about things between us from other times. All of the faces were familiar, my mother, teachers from school, the social worker who used to take me to the hospital, the first girl I kissed, many others I had tried to love, but not Bernice.

The dream meant nothing to me except perhaps that in my life there was no order. Today, however, there will be order. There are things to do, people to see.

Bernice stirs beside me.

"What time is it, Joe?"

"I dunno, six or seven."

"The clock's there."

"Quarter after seven. Time to get up. Gonna be a big day."

"Ah, not yet, Joe, come hold me."

Her arms snake up from under the blankets and coil around me. I feel myself being crushed. She is like a python and I see myself being swallowed whole and becoming a lump in her stomach.

I slid away.

"Hey!"

"Com'on, up and at 'em kid, a new day."

"Joe," she calls, but I'm gone. I have the shower running and the water and soap form a slick seal around my body. I think of it as armour. Lifebuoy soap to give me 24-hour protection. Days when nothing can touch me I'm at my best.

I hear her brushing her teeth.

"Joe," she says, "can we take the kids to the Ex'?"

"Is it open?"

"It opened Friday."

The Canadian National Exhibition. Opening on the day of my release. I might have been able to get a job there as a freak or something. No, I don't have enough quality. Still it's funny.

"How's the money?" I ask.

"How much have you got left?"

"About a hundred."

"I've got almost $40 in the bank," she says.

"Yeah, but what about rent and all that? You're cut off from your allowance, aren't you?"

"My worker said I might get one more cheque. The Welfare'll give us something. We'll have enough. You might hear from that job today too."

"I've got to see my parole guy today," I say.

It's quiet for a moment. The tap is still running but she's stopped brushing.

"Can I come?" she asks.

I think about it. Shame is a private thing. It's even harder to share than love and yet I wonder about the shame that's in me, if it's really that or a reluctance to open a door into myself. I'm more fearful than Old Mother Hubbard who went to the cupboard. I'm afraid the emptiness will be discovered and fill the shelves with pretend things like shame.

"Sure, if you want," I say.

"What time is it for?"

"Eleven, but one of us has gotta be here for the Welfare."

"Oh, they usually come early," she says. "They love to catch you in bed."

We laugh.

And then the kids are awake and filling up the small room. Bernice is telling them about going to the Exhibition. There's a lot of excited squealing and I fill my ears with shampoo, but I can't say I'm unhappy.

After breakfast the kids go out to play. Bernice cleans and washes and I begin to cut out the pieces of leather for the purses I promised to make. If I work quickly I'll be able to begin stitching tomorrow.

Bernice brings me a cup of coffee and then runs the vacuum-cleaner near my feet. I hear her clinking all the empty bottles into the garbage in the kitchen and she's walking over my head tidying the rooms upstairs.

About ten there's a rap on the door. I answer it. A woman stands there smiling fiercely. Her hair is brown and long with streaks of gold in it. She has a well sun-tanned face with blue eyes that don't look straight out but rather to the side. She's much younger than Bernice or me.

"I'm Miss Cultiss," she says.

"Com'on in."

She hesitates and begins to explain. "From the Department of Welfare. I'm looking for Mr. and Mrs. Cross."

"That's me," I say. "Mr. Cross."

"Oh yes, of course." Her smile works hard.

I lead her to the living-room and sit her down. Bernice pops her head in.

"I'll make coffee," she says.

"Oh, not for me," the woman says. "I mean, don't make

it specially for me."

"I want some anyway," I say.

"That's fine then. I'll just have it black."

She's wearing a short skirt, which is the biggest worry on her mind right now. She's sitting directly across from me and any position she takes allows me an unobstructed view of her long legs. So she won't tear her skirt to shreds trying to lengthen it for the occasion I move back behind the small table where the leather's being cut. She is to one side of me now and this seems to make her more comfortable.

"You do leather work," she says.

"Yeah, I learned it in prison. Kind of a hobby to pass the time."

"I hear you can make good money at it too," she says, and her eyes blink innocently.

"I guess, if you're good at it. I'm not very good yet."

"Is that how you plan to make your living now, Mr. Cross?"

"No, if it was we'd starve."

Bernice brings in the coffee and sits down quietly.

"This is my wife," I say.

The woman stands up and drops her papers. I pick them up and she sits down again, a determined look on her face.

"Now," she says. "You filled out the application in the office so there's no need to go over that unless anything's changed." Her eyes lift and dart sideways.

"Not in one day," I say. "Everything's the same."

"I see here, Mrs. Cross, you were receiving the Mother's Allowance."

"Yes," Bernice says, "but when Joe got parole, the parole people told Mother's Allowance and they said now it was up to Joe to look after us."

"So they won't be sending any more?"

"No."

"Who's your worker there, please? You see, I just have to check." Her voice is getting firmer now, things are settling into the pattern she's used to.

Bernice tells her the name of the woman who is her worker.

"Didn't you receive some money from the penitentiary when you were released, Mr. Cross?"

"Yeah, I did."

"What happened to that? I mean, it's only been. . . ." She consults her papers.

"Five days," I say.

"Yes, five days. Surely you must have some of that left."

I look at her hard. I wish now I hadn't moved. I should have kept her squirming.

"Do you know how much I got when I was released?"

"Well no, but still . . . ."

"I got next to nothing, and you know what I did when I got out?" Her eyes are alert and they've moved closer together.

"I don't have any idea."

"Well, I went wild. I went right crazy and went out and bought some groceries. And then I bought myself some shoes and a new shirt and and even a new pair of pants. And then while I still had some left I went really berserk and had a small celebration with my wife, who I haven't seen for five years. So, you see, now I'm broke. I know I should have been more careful, but that was never one of my strong points."

Her long hands with their pointed fingernails are fidgeting with her pen. She looks as if she's trying to decide something. She pushes her legs back hard against the chair and pulls her body up straight. Her eyes are in their separate orbits again.

"Well you'll certainly have to learn to budget a little better than that," she says.

I find it hard not to smile. We live in a world that has nothing wrong in it, only the individual himself makes a mistake and is responsible if things go wrong in his life. In prison they taught us that over and over again; if you ended up in the hole because you refused to cut grass it was your own fault. There was nothing wrong with the job of cutting grass, in fact it was a privilege, you got to see the people from the outside when they came to visit. All those nice young girls with their skirts blowing in the wind.

And my friend who hanged himself because life imprisonment was a time beyond his comprehension was called weak by the prison officials. Even the prison priest refused to bury him.

So this silly young woman was nothing new. In fact she was a familiar joke.

"I'm pretty good at that," Bernice says.

The woman smiles gratefully.

"I guess that's all then," she says. "You should get a cheque in several days that will cover you for two weeks. If you're not working by then, Mr. Cross, and need further assistance you'll have to re-apply at the office." And then she stands, smoothing her skirt up under her. She is a pretty woman with large, tough-looking breasts. Her belly hasn't been swollen with children and would probably be a pleasure to lie against, but I think only of the word bitch and I want to ask her if she has a cat.

"Thank you," she says, moving toward the door.

"It's been great fun," I say in what I hope is an ambiguous tone.

And then she looks at me, very straight and direct. It's frightening to see so much hate in a young person's eyes. It's like the prison myth that the old screws are the worst when in fact it's the young ones that are the most brutal. The hate of the young is a new thing and has more strength in it to hurt you.

"I'll show you to the door," Bernice says and the woman goes.

She makes me wonder again about all the people in my life who have been paid to help me.

Bernice is laughing when she returns. I'm back cutting leather.

"You really gave her a hard time," she says.

"She tried to give us a hard time."

"Well, she's pretty young. Anyway we got it."

122

"Yeah," but I'm thinking how much something like that could cost. What happens to people who have to spend their whole lives dealing with people like that? I guess in their own minds they become prisoners. Nobody. They used to stand outside the classification officer's door or even Deek's. And they'd knock timidly and someone behind the door would say, Who is it? And they'd answer, Nobody, just me. And they'd give their number.

"We should go soon for the parole interview," Bernice says.

"Yeah, I just thought I haven't reported to the police yet either."

"You have to do that?"

"Every month."

"Maybe we should take a taxi so we're not late." Her face is worried. She's used to worrying about other people's time.

"Let's walk. It's a nice day. It doesn't matter if we're late. He's not going anywhere."

We hold hands on the street. The kids see us and run over.

"Where ya goin'?" Lucy asks.

"We've got an appointment," Bernice says. "We won't be long though and when we come back we'll all go to the Exhibition."

"Can I go on all the rides?" Lucy is asking and then she and Cathy get into an argument about what rides are best. We drift away from them.

It's not a long walk but I'm surprised how tired I am when we arrive. I'm not used to having so much space to move around in and my body is no longer trained for such big movements.

It's a big building and we have to take an elevator to reach the office. When I tell the secretary my name she informs me that I'm late.

"Yes," I say.

"Take a seat then. You'll have to wait."

It's only the usual few minutes and then a young thin man

appears and opens the gate so we can come behind the counter.

"My office is down there," he says, pointing. His voice is thin too. He moves very quickly and has already sat down as I begin to introduce Bernice.

"This is my wife, Bernice. . . ."

He rockets to his feet and his long arm flashes past my face toward Bernice, who seems for a second about to jump out of its way.

He strikes me as a nervous man.

"I'm Bruce Nesbitt," he says, smiling brightly, but when this is met with silence he frowns down at his desk and moves some papers around. We wait patiently and eventually his tight face becomes radiant again. "And you're Joe Cross?"

"Yes."

"Well, how are you?"

It's a temptation to tell him. My moods change so quickly. The other woman has left me feeling mad and hard. He'd be an easy person to hurt and that's a temptation too.

"Fine, I'm fine."

"And how are things . . . I mean, how are you making out?"

Making out? Jeezus. . . .

"Fine. Everything's great."

"I'm new here," he says, standing up and facing the window with his back to us. Perhaps he's just shy. "There's a lot of guys I've met who figure because I'm their supervisor they can't talk to me. You know, tell me anything. If you're having trouble or anything. . . . I mean I'm here to help you the best I can."

"Sure," I say, and he turns around.

"I don't know what it was like there for you," he says, "but it's all in the past now, right?"

"Sure." I don't blame him for not wanting to hear about it.

"What are your thoughts, Mrs. Cross?"

Bernice looks a bit startled.

"I just don't want Joe to go back."

He's still standing, but now he sits down and looks very intently at her.

"I don't think there's any danger of that. From the reports I'd say Joe is a pretty intelligent guy. There are a few rules he has to obey. Rules that probably you can help with. One of the most serious stipulations is against drinking, other than. . . ."

"But that's stupid," Bernice says. "Joe likes to have a drink. It's not fair to hold that over his head."

"It's not being held over his head," he says. "It's meant to help Joe."

She says nothing. I'm examining the ceiling quite closely.

"Have you had any luck with a job?" he asks.

"There's a good chance the place where I used to work will take me back."

"Well, that's marvelous. That's sort of the main thing. I mean, once you get working it's so much easier to get back into the swing of things, don'tcha think?"

I agreed. It was all a formula. A generation of formula-eaters. We wouldn't know a tit full of real milk if it squirted us in the eye. So now all I had to do was supply the right ingredients as he asked for them. Just the right proportion of ingredients for him to make a report that all was well.

"And how are the two of you . . . I mean are things working out for the two of you? And you have . . . " peeking at his papers now, "two children. Are they having any difficulties?"

"There are some things," Bernice says.

I'm surprised.

"It was never perfect between us anyway," she says. "And while Joe was away, things happened. We both got mad at each other. It'll take us a while to get all that straight."

"The main thing," he says, standing again, "is you're willing to try."

"Yes," she says.

"And you Joe?"

"Sure." But what has occurred to me is that I don't have

125

any choice. I'd like to say this but I think they'd both get angry, though for different reasons.

"Well," he says, making a note in a book, "why don't you drop in to see me next week? Say the same time?"

"Alright, but if I get a job I'll call you. Okay?"

"Well certainly, that comes first. We can always arrange another time and if anything comes up in the meantime that I can help with please call me."

"Thanks," I say as he shakes my hand and then Bernice's.

"It's been nice meeting you, Mrs. Cross," he says. "And you, Joe."

"See you," I say.

We leave quickly and outside the hot sun dries the sweat off me.

"You want to walk?" Bernice asks.

"Yes." And I'm thinking, today it's Tuesday and tomorrow it'll be Wednesday and then Thursday. Finally it'll be Friday again, a week from when I started. My first anniversary and my mind swells up and bursts past that Friday and spills over into the next and the next. And I see my life as a kind of waiting for Fridays, each one a mark, a gold attendance star. Perhaps a renewal. A religion. I'll be like an old lady eagerly awaiting Sundays so she can scurry off to church in her best clothes to pay homage to a God who has left her abandoned. My day of worship will be Friday.

"It wasn't so bad," Bernice says. "He was pretty nice."

"I've met worse."

"He seemed really interested. Like he wanted to help."

"The funny thing is he probably does."

She stops walking and looks at me closely, but I'm no longer there. I'm calculating the number of Fridays left in my life.

"Why is that funny?"

Maybe a thousand. Maybe 2000.

"Because he can't do anything," I say. "Not for me. He certainly can't do anything for me unless I let him and then it's me doing him a favour."

126

We're walking again, holding hands, and she turns her smiling face toward me.

"You've sure got some screwy ideas," she says.

The sun is hot on my head and in my mind. Behind the shadows of my memory I see a desert. I was there once years ago. It's outside of Winnipeg, about a hundred miles south of the city. The army uses it to test artillery. I always thought a desert would be like a prison and now I know I was wrong.

There was a path leading from the road and every few feet signs warned of the danger. For some reason I didn't care. The air was dry and gentle in my lungs. I didn't bother to smoke. I kept walking and after several miles the brush got thinner and thinner and finally there was only the sand. I leaped from the top of the sliding hills and rolled softly into the sandy valleys. I scrambled up the rises, my hands grabbing fistfuls of the sand that held me.

Hardly anything grew there, a bit of sage-brush and some pale pink flowers, tiny things with long thin roots. I walked an hour in the sand and then turned around and came back. Later I was surprised I hadn't got lost. Now I think I understand why.

In prison I had a number. 3274. I lived in a numbered cell-block. My cell was marked with black paint, D-4. In prison though there was a sameness to things and it was easy to get dislocated, if, say, the wrong-numbered clothes were issued. There was no arguing the point. A notation was made in the wrong file and an explanation was demanded for something you knew nothing about. Reluctant admissions of guilt and lies became the order of the day. And after a sleeping pill or two it was easy to find the wrong bed. It was hardly noticed.

But in the desert there were no reference points. There was no phone-booth to call someone from and say, Meet me at the corner of Dundas and Yonge. There were no markers. If you were asked to give your location the only answer was here. There were no clocks. Without a clock the only time was now.

Perhaps because the desert is sand it doesn't remember

anything. It's like a child that doesn't remember yesterday. It doesn't plan for tomorrow. There are no landmarks like Christmas, Easter and summer holidays. There's nothing solid to hang out. The shape of each moment is scattered by the wind. In the end the final thing is space.

In prison I remembered, and waited. I even got permission to wear a watch. My heart barely beat and when I thought of movement it came to me as a shadowy image of a figure running.

I was often lost in prison but it was easy for me to find my way again. In the desert I didn't even have my own footprints to follow. I became my own search party and was never out of touch.

"What're you thinking?" she asks.

"About how hard it'd be to build snowmen in the desert."

"Really!"

"Really."

The sun makes her eyes squint and when we talk she slows down to look at me. I wonder if my face has changed in five years. I might even be a different person. I am in fact because she's different. I haven't yet made the adjustment. She has to keep checking my credentials. Maybe at night she takes out the old photographs. Sometimes at night when she thinks I'm sleeping I feel her hands searching my body. She may discover someday that I'm an impostor.

"What was it like?" she says.

"What?"

"You know. In there."

"Oh in there. Well. . . ."

"I mean, if you want to talk about it."

"I don't mind," I say, and I don't. I like to think about it. It's more familiar than this.

"In Kingston they kept the windows open and the place was full of birds. In the morning they'd start chirpin' about six and just about drive you nuts. After a while though you got used to them. It got so I used to lie awake early waiting for them."

The birds were good things. The flutter of their wings

made it easier to accept the flutter in my chest that came some mornings when I felt scared about nothing. That's how it seemed some mornings, as if there was nothing, but then there were the birds who had chosen for some reason to build their nests along the heating pipes across from our cells and you could watch their lives grow as eggs hatched and the young birds learned to fly. In the summer the cleaners swept up at least half a dozen of the young birds who'd fallen and died. These were natural accidents of life, but once a young man, compelled perhaps by the sight of the birds or some inner desire to be free, jumped from the fourth tier and his smashed body was covered with a sheet that slowly stained red as we marched past to get our breakfast trays.

"Did anybody ever make friends with them?"

I laugh.

"No, there was no bird-man of Alcatraz."

"Did anybody ever bother you? You know, you hear those stories."

"Queers? Sure. The second day I got there a guy started sending me notes, and then cigarettes and candy. Said he wanted me to be his kid."

"What happened?"

"Well, I finally met him and it turned out he was nineteen, just a kid himself, spent most of his life in training schools and reformatories. He was just lonely. He wanted a friend but most guys won't admit that and they go through a lot of crap about trying to make another guy their kid so they'll have somebody around they can depend on."

"Did anything happen?"

"No. I told him I wasn't interested and after a while we got to be friends."

Except he was so alone in his mind, so lost and afraid he needed the touch of another person to anchor him to wherever he was. He sat beside me sometimes in the movies and his hand always reached out for mine. It was a tough, thick-skinned hand that he would squeeze over mine so hard that I was bruised. I never understood his hard hands or how they got that way. He worked in the kitchen cutting meat, a job I didn't think would give you callouses. He had green eyes, very soft and gentle. They made me think of spring grass bright with the early-morning dew. I wondered how his hands and eyes were connected, if what he touched was the same as what he saw. He stabbed a boy younger than himself in the kitchen one day. It wasn't a bad wound and the boy bragged about the scar on his face later and my friend was given electric-shock treatment and placed in an isolation ward.

"Did anybody else try?"

"Not really. I'm not exactly the baby-face type and anyway it's the kind of place where if you have some respect for yourself people leave you alone."

"Weren't you scared, Joe?"

"Sometimes I was, when I thought about dying."

She's quiet now, her hand sweaty in mine. She's the only woman I know whose hands sweat like mine. She is the only woman whose hand I'm not embarrassed to hold.

This morning it's raining slightly. Just a drizzle really. I folded my tent wet and walked to the station to wait for the train. I've been travelling a week now and I'm a long way from home.

Home. Home is where the heart is, someone said. Home is where you hang your hat. There are a lot of expressions like that. None of them quite fits how I feel though. Home to me is more like that story in the Bible where this guy asks his father for his share of the family estate and then takes off to the city and spends the money on wine, women and song; and when it's all gone and he's really down and out he decides to go home and sure enough his father is waiting and forgives him.

So for some people home is where you go back to get forgiven so you can start over.

I'm standing in this small northern Ontario train station waiting for a train to take me even farther north. North from Toronto. But hundreds of miles south three figures stand waiting in my memory, their eyes watching me from different angles, their mouths shaping a single word, a simple word but it's like an accusation, a verdict of guilty and a long prison sentence all rolled into one: Hey, they say. Hey! That's all. But I'm gone. I don't need to be forgiven. I'm a free man.

"Hey!" someone shouts. "Hey, fairy."

And I turn, but before I can see who it is this huge guy grabs me and is swinging me around like I'm a favourite toy that's been lost and found again.

I drop my pack-sack. He bends over to retrieve it and then I see his face. It's like the face of a friendly camel, but it looks familiar.

"Ya remember, don'tcha?" he says.

I rake through the images in my past, but there's no name to go with this big hump of a man.

"Wayne," he says. "Wayne Flamont. From D.B. Hood school. 'Member?"

I begin to say a reluctant No but it's too late, he's turned away from me and is signalling a woman across the room.

She moves toward us slowly, working her way through the crowd. She's a pretty woman except she has no shine. It's as if the rain has washed away her smile. And her eyes, a pale, pale blue, are like that of an air traveller's who's come too far too fast. She makes me think of long distances, of height, of mountains. Her hair, long and thick in different shades of brown, reminds me of the branches of a tree blowing in the wind on some faraway slope, so far away you can only dream of touching them.

"This is Doris," Wayne says. "My wife. Can ya believe it, we're on our bloody honeymoon."

And then he laughs and his big body shakes, but I've noticed with people that there are two ways a body can react when you laugh—it can expand and get looser and there's the real joy of letting go, or it can scrunch itself up and get tighter as if what's being laughed about isn't funny at all.

Wayne's laugh draws his body in like the bellows of an accordion and his mouth gives off a choking sound as if something is caught in his wind-pipe.

"I'm Joe," I say. "Joe Cross."

And she takes my hand politely and her soft skin burns against mine.

"We useta go to the same school," he says. "Christ, about a hundred years ago, eh Joe?"

"The train's loading," she says. "We'd better get on."

"Sure," he says. And he moves off with my pack. "Com'on Joe, we'll treatcha to breakfast."

And so I follow, unsure of why I'm here or where I'm going.

We find seats across from each other in the same car. Wayne heaves our luggage onto the overhead racks and we head for the dining-car. Perhaps it's lucky that I've met these people. There's a six-hour trip ahead of us, though the distance is only 180 miles. It's a slow trip, the train stopping at every little outpost, even stopping to pick up Indians or fishermen who flag it down. It could be a boring trip without someone to talk to.

We order breakfast and then sit waiting.

"So how come you're up this way?" Wayne asks.

"Running away," I say honestly.

And he laughs again and nudges Doris, who is systematically tearing her cigarette package apart. She reminds me of Cathy, my daughter, ten years old, scared and always hiding inside something, her colouring books, the TV, sometimes just chewing on her upper lip, her eyes glazed over. When I was a little kid there was a popular song about whistling in the dark when you were scared. If you whistled the scared feeling went away. It was my favourite song for a long time but now I can't remember the words or even the tune, but I have this feeling that I'd like to nudge Doris too and ask, Hey, know any good songs, and she'd sort of jerk up out of her dream and say, well the one I like best is ...and she'd start off and Wayne and I would join in and then he'd tell us his favourite and before you'd know it we'd all be remembering our happiest songs, and singing them and feeling close to each other like people should. Like real friends.

"I remember that time when you really did run away," Wayne says. "Around grade six I think. Your picture was in all the papers and your mother was on the radio asking you to come home. I betcha forgot about that, eh?"

"No. I stayed away for almost a week. I slept one night in a graveyard."

"Why did you run away?" Doris asks.

I try to remember. Her face is watching me carefully. It's more open now, like a flower that has been in the sun after a long darkness.

"I lost something and I was scared to go home."

"What did you lose?" she asks.

I think. "Oh I know. My paper-route money." And suddenly I remember Wayne as he was then, twenty years ago, one of the boys in a gang I wanted to join so badly I let them use me as a toy. "You used to hang around with Ted Birchill and those guys, didn't you? I mean it was sort of a gang."

"Yeah, we were regular little bastards," Wayne says.

The waitress brings our breakfast. The train is moving foward slowly, rocking us back and forth. In my mind I'm standing in the middle of a circle of boys who are laughing and shouting at me. I'm eleven years old, a small thin nervous boy who is trying to be a good sport. Fairy hairy face, they say, fairy hairy face. Whatcha got in the bag fairy hairy, more bobby-pins for yer hair? And the other kids laugh. It's a good joke. My mother loves my hair and won't let me get it cut. It's so long in the front she pins it up in the morning before I leave the house. Of course I take out the bobby-pin but then my hair hangs in my face. And all the kids know about the bobby-pins anyway. Maybe he's got his lunch in the bag, one of the boys says. Yeah, toad-jelly sandwiches. And they laugh. No, no, says another, that's toe-jam sandwiches. They're having a good time but of course they're wrong about the paper bag I'm holding. It doesn't contain my lunch or bobby-pins either but the week's collection from my paper route. I shake the bag so they can hear the coins jingle. They become quiet and I feel them in my power. It's a wonderful feeling. Well, what's in it? one of the bigger boys asks. Com'on fairy, tell us. But now I'm sort of dancing and shaking the bag like a maraca. The circle is getting larger and larger. More kids come to watch. I feel like a hero, like a pitcher who has struck out the home-run hitter in the last inning, or like a football player who has caught the pass that wins the game, and the crowd is roaring. They love me. I've given them a special feeling. I'm yelling like a medicine-man who has brought on the rain everyone has been waiting for. And then suddenly the bag breaks. The coins are flying everywhere and the kids are all grabbing at them. I stand there stunned, my glory dance is over. I'm forgotten already. And then I remember the money and I'm on my knees too. I recover a couple of dollars but there were over twelve in the bag, a few bills but mostly change, and now its gone. I don't care though. It was worth it. I want to shout that at the boys who are running away: I don't care! But I don't say anything because I'm scared. When my mother finds out she'll come to the school and speak to the principal, who'll call me in and ask the names of the boys who took the money. And then everyone will hate me. So I decide right then not to go home.

The coffee is served and we're all smoking cigarettes.

"Seriously Joe," Wayne said. "What're you doing up this way?"

I look at his wide face, it's an open, honest face; hard to imagine a face like that scaring me.

"I told you, I'm sort of running away."

"A vacation, you mean?"

"Sort of."

"Well, what've you been doing all these years? I never heard anything about you. Teddy Birchill, you know, went in the army, didn't even finish high school. And Jack Rogers has a good job at the Morris Hotel right across from where I work."

"What do you do?" I ask.

"I'm assistant manager at the Canadian Tire store at Yonge and Davenport. You know the place."

"Sure," I say.

"That's where I met Doris too. She came in to buy a hose or something and there I was."

We all sort of chuckle at this.

"What do you do Doris?" I ask.

"I'm a nurse," she says. "Mostly private. I don't like big hospitals."

"I don't blame you. They're pretty impersonal."

"You get lost in them," she says.

"She's really something to have around to take your pulse," Wayne says. "It's a real pleasure to get sick."

And she reaches across the table and squeezes his hand. He smiles secretly at her and her eyes seem to laugh and then turn away to watch the trees flashing by.

"So how long have you guys been married?" I ask, because suddenly I feel excluded. Their gestures of affection have sent me back to my prison cell. Like when I was a kid and my father would sometimes say: go to your room. Not because he was mad at me. Nothing like that except he pretended to be. He wanted to be alone with my mother, that's all.

"Ten days," Wayne says. "We got married at old Holy Trinity. You know, downtown, and then we went to Niagara Falls. Took the bus and stayed at the International. We did the whole thing, you know, the ferry, walking under the Falls. The whole thing, Even went to Buffalo."

"It was terrible," Doris says, and she's laughing.

"We had fun," he says smugly, "and now we're gonna end up with a couple of days in God's country."

The dishes are cleared and we order more coffee.

"Well," Wayne says, "we've told you everything. What about you? Where've you been? What've you been doing?"

Pussy cat, pussy cat where've you been?
I've been to London to visit the Queen.

"There's not much to it," I say, and I guess really there isn't. "After school I got a job and then I got married, had a kid and then another one. You know."

"You with kids!" Wayne says. "So where are they?"

"In Toronto with their mother."

"Wow!" he says. "I never really imagined you with kids and all that. So how is it? Maybe you can give Doris and me some pointers."

I want to laugh out loud, slap him on the back, except Doris is watching me like a judge waiting for the truth.

"Well, the thing is, Wayne, a few years ago I just got bored with everything. I mean I was doing okay, good job repairing cameras, not making a bad buck but I got bored."

"Yeah, that happens to me too. Sometimes you wonder why you're doing everything. Until you meet someone like Doris." And he looks at her in a kind of loving, longing way.

"So you did something," Doris says.

"Yeah. I robbed a bank."

136

Our bodies move closer like the poles of a tepee to form a shelter.

"And then you went to jail?" Doris asks.

"Yeah, I got twelve years but they gave me parole so I was only there around four."

"Holy shit!" Wayne says.

"So how long you been . . . ?"

"A couple of weeks. Probably just about the time you guys were getting married I was getting out."

"So what'll you do now?" Wayne asks.

The same question.

"I thought I'd go home but that was no good."

"I guess things change," Doris says. "I mean I don't go home much, just at Christmas usually and it's always hard. We're like strangers. There's nothing to talk about except the things they remember."

"Things change," I say, "but I figure that's the way it should be. I don't know how to explain it except I don't feel bad about anything."

I'm talking to Doris because I think maybe she'll understand. I didn't want to tell them about the prison thing because I thought they'd feel sorry for me and when people do that it's a dead end. It's hard then to tell them how happy you are just being with them, that everything really is okay.

"I look on it as an experience," I say. "Something that most people don't have. I'm lucky in a way. I mean it's something to talk about that's better than Niagara Falls."

Doris laughs and for a brief moment I'm the secret dancer in her eyes.

Wayne has a worried look. "What about a job though? I've heard it's really hard to get a job after . . . that, you know. And your family."

"I feel like it's going to be okay," I say, and I do. "It's like coming out of a long sleep, it takes a while to wake up, but when I do things'll turn out okay."

"Is that why you came up here?" Doris asks, "to wake up?"

"Why did you come up?" I ask.

"We thought it'd be different," Wayne says.

"Me too."

Our coffee is gone again. It's almost noon. People are beginning to come in for lunch. The train speeds up, then slows down and stops to discharge and pick up passengers. Wayne plays nervously with his empty cup, banging it against the empty saucer. Doris is studying me from behind the cloud of smoke from her cigarette.

"Maybe we should go back to our seats," Wayne says. "Probably somebody'll want our table."

"That sounds like a good idea," I say. "I think I'll take a nap." I feel very tired. And then as we stand up Doris reaches over and shakes my hand. It still feels very hot.

"I'm so glad we met you," she says. "It's been a real pleasure."

And then Wayne too is shaking my hand. "Me too Joe, I'm really glad we met ya."

And it's like they are saying good-bye though the trip won't be over for hours. Perhaps, I think, for some of us there's only so much we can say to each other. And I think of that crazy prison song somebody always sang at our concerts: down every road there's always one more city, and then the guy sings: and the highway is my home. It's like some people settle forever and ever in one of those cities and they like to be visited by the people that are passing through but if they settled down next door things would be awkward. Being so close, I guess they have to face the fact that they are strangers.

I stall around the counter getting cigarettes and when I get back to my seat they are lying wrapped together, arms around each other, eyes closed, perhaps sleeping. I slide into my seat across the aisle and stare out the window.

The trees flash by like fingers on a hand waving. And I think of that last day at home, leaving, getting into the cab and two floors above me, standing on the balcony, Bernice, Cathy and Lucy, waving. Send us a postcard, Cathy yelled. Yeah, Lucy said, her face pressed between the bars of the railing, send us somethin'.

138

There had been no crying. The night before when Bernice asked if I would be back I answered as honestly as I could. If it feels right, I'd said.

It's summer and the trees are fully leaved. We're travelling faster now and it's hard to concentrate on an individual tree for more than a second. The leaves are hiding the secrets of the forest under a blanket of yellows and greens. I wonder about the blackness that lies beyond the edge of the forest. The dark core where the leaves have almost no colour. And I think, the leaves are the fingerprints of the trees, but in the fall they drop off and rot on the ground. And in the spring there are new leaves, new fingerprints as if the trees were reborn. It's sort of a joke in my mind, imagining the RCMP trying to keep track of the fingerprints of the trees. I guess men are easier to catch.

The train has stopped again and people are moving around me.

"We're here," Wayne says, and he swings my pack down. I'm still groggy from sleep.

"Moosonee," he says. "We're here. Hey look, we've gotta rush. We're staying at the Riverlit Lodge, so come and see us, eh?"

"Sure, sure." But we both know I won't. It would be an intrusion.

"Bye," Doris says. "Hope you wake up, you know, and enjoy yourself."

"Bye," I say.

I wait for the train to clear. I'm too tired to be patient with a crowd.

I'm here because I've heard the place is still a frontier town. Also there's a provincial park on an island. This is my final destination. The island. I'll spend one night and go back on the train in the morning.

The station is small, an old wooden building with long wooden benches. There's a cigarette machine with an out-of-order sign hung on it and a soft-drink machine where I buy a Coke that's warm and too sweet.

I ask an old Indian where I get the boat for the island and

he points to the end of the street, where I can see the grey water of the river.

The sun is very hot. I wish I had a hat. The pack slaps against my back and I begin to sweat and feel the tiredness spreading through me. It's crazy being here like this when I could be sitting at home in the shade of the balcony with a cold beer in my hand.

It seems a simple town to understand at first glance. The streets are full of Indians. They are all walking, shuffling really, some of them staggering. The cars on the street are all driven by white people—young women in light cotton dresses, their hair fluffy and soft looking. They are intent on their business of shopping and keeping appointments. The Indians look unconcerned, shiftless. And I think of a phrase I've heard somewhere: unsuitable for employment. Or maybe just unsuitable.

This is a town with a growing tourist industry, I've heard. Most of the native people work at the pulp-and-paper mills. There's a bit of mining going on too, asbestos I think. It'd be an easy place to live. Everything is clearcut. The natives walk, and the others drive along in their Japanese imports or get picked up in the Ford station-waggons sent out from the resorts to greet the tourists.

Just like prison in a way. The wheels and the goofs. Sort of black and white.

I buy a ticket at the dock, but the man tells me the next boat won't be leaving for an hour so I stash my things in his shack and head up the hill to find a beer.

There's no beverage room so I sit in the dining-room, where I have to order a hamburger to get a beer.

"Sorry," the girl says. "It's the rules."

"That's okay," I tell her and we both laugh because we know it's not.

The place is full. Supper-hour I guess. I sip at the beer and let my eyes wander around the room. People aren't very interesting when they're eating, but directly to my left there are four people who are waiting to be served and are talking hard. Well, three of them are.

There's a man, his wife and daughter and a young man, certainly not a son so I assume he's a boy friend of the daughter's. She's maybe twenty.

The young man is sitting beside the mother. He's wearing a black suit, a white shirt and a red tie. He's talking loudly but I can't make out the words, just that the noise is loud and he's waving his arms and gesturing toward the girl who seems to be ignoring them all.

I can't see the girl too clearly because her father is in the way, but when he leans forward I catch glimpses of her. She looks quite a bit overweight. In profile she has several chins. Her hair is the colour of muddy water and has the texture of steel wool. Not a raving beauty but there's a friendly sloppiness about her that I like. As if she doesn't care about any of this. While the others talk she's straining her fat neck to see around the room. It's not as if she's nervous or has lost something. It's hard to describe except I know I do it myself a lot, it's sort of like looking for someone or something worth giving your attention to.

I like her, three chins and all.

The girl's mother grabs her arm to try and focus her attention on the conversation. The girl turns and for a split second we're looking into each other's eyes. And she seems to smile. I know I am. Like we have a secret. Like friends do when things are too busy to allow them time to stop and talk.

The waitress brings another beer and I check the time. I have to go soon and besides the food has arrived at the other table and everyone is eating except the young man, who is still talking. I feel sorry for him. I wish I could send him a note saying something like: forget it, relax. It wouldn't work though. He looks so hungry, with his neatly trimmed hair, so desperate. He unfolds his napkin, places it across his lap and begins to eat politely. The other three are bent over their plates, shovelling the food in. Perhaps her parents have money.

The boat is waiting for passengers at the dock. I hand in my ticket and explain to the man I need to be picked up at seven in order to catch the train at eight.

He grins, an Indian. "Not much time," he says. "One night."

"Enough," I say.

"Lots a black flies and mosquitoes," he says. "Better have plenty of stuff for them or there won't be nothin' left fur me to pick up in the morning."

The other Indians in the boat laugh. The only other white people in the big canoe are a young couple with packs who seem scared.

The young man asks me: "Are you camping on the island tonight?"

"Yeah, and I'm going back in the morning."

"We're staying a week," he says, and then he looks at his girl. "We plan a week anyway."

The Indians laugh louder and the boat moves out.

As soon as we reach the other shore I ask the boatman to let me out. He stops and I get out quickly before the young couple decide that this is where they should get out too. The boatman, as if sensing my desire to be alone, pulls away the second my foot is out of the boat.

"See you at seven," he shouts. And the young couple wave at me. What the hell, I think and I wave back.

I climb the ten or twelve feet to the top of the embankment, find a small clearing among some pines and pitch my tent. I roll out my sleeping bag to let it air, and then I dig a small pit to build a fire in.

I dreamed of doing these simple things when I was in prison. I realize now that I made myself a promise that I would do them. They mean nothing in themselves except that I am here and there's no-one else to approve or disapprove of what I'm doing.

I cook some wieners on the fire, eat them off the stick and watch the shadows grow. I feel wonderfully alone. Even the bugs seem to have had their fill of me. I think I know how a wise man must feel, how it must feel to be God, issuing orders, giving commands. I mean, why should anyone listen to someone telling them what to do once they realize that they're totally on their own anyway?

And I'm laughing into the darkness like an animal and it's so good just to hear my own voice. Somewhere else maybe God is laughing too.

A wind has come up, a cold wind from the wide river, so I piss into the fire and go into the tent to the warmth of my sleeping-bag. I fall asleep with nothing on my mind, not even sex.

I'm woken by a tapping on the tent. It's raining. I get up and dress quickly. It's only a little after six but I don't want to miss my boat. There's an anxiety in me again to get going. I'm still not sure where. I have to do something though. I have almost no money left. No more train rides after this one. Strictly my thumb. And if I don't head back to Toronto I'll have to get a job soon just to eat.

I break camp and wait under the trees. The rain is soft like a mist but it's thick and a few minutes in it and I'd be soaked. I forgot to bring a raincoat.

The boatman is ten minutes early. He throws me a yellow slicker to put over my head and we roar off toward the opposite shore. At the dock he speaks to another Indian who has an old half-ton truck.

"He'll give ya a ride," he says.

I thank him and give him a dollar, which he holds in his hand until it's slick from the rain.

"It's a favour," he says finally and hands me back the bill.

"Thanks," is all I can think of to say. I feel foolish but then I hold out my hand and he shakes it and grins at me.

"Go," he says, and I run up to the waiting truck.

At the station the driver stops and holds his hand out palm up and I give him the wet dollar. He grunts and I sort of laugh because that's the way life is, I mean full of crazy surprises.

The station is jammed with people and the place has the smell of wet clothing to it. Babies are crying, and people are trying to sleep on the benches. I buy another Coke from the machine and it's still warm and sticky sweet. And I see the family. The mother in a plain line dress to distract from

143

her size, light blue raincoat slung over one arm and a matching purse. The father is wearing a tan-coloured suit, nicely tailored, solid middle management, and this morning, as he talks business with the young man who is still trapped inside his black suit, white shirt and red tie, he's wearing a sporty brown fedora. They nudge each other and occasionally laugh as if their business is finished and they can relax. Except they still seem tense and their eyes dart around the room as if they were looking for something they've lost. The girl isn't with them so they don't interest me much. I wonder if they've left her behind, but that doesn't seem like them. I mean her parents have obviously fattened her to take her to market.

I wander over to the front of the station to avoid getting crushed as the loading begins. And then I see her. She's walking back and forth on the wooden platform. Not walking, skipping really and she has nothing to protect her from the rain. She isn't wearing a coat and her dress with all its crinolines hangs from her like a deflated balloon. Her hair is pasted to her head and it looks like she's wearing a hat made of dead weeds. And her mouth is moving as she skips along. Christ, the crazy broad is singing.

I go to the front door and yell at her. "Hey, you're gonna get pneumonia out there."

But she just keeps moving along and she's singing: Raindrops are falling on my head / and just like a guy whose feet are too big for him / then nothing seems to fit / those raindrops are falling on my head / they keep falling / so I just did me some talking to the sun / and I said I didn't like the way / he got things done. . . .

"Hey!" I say. "Com'on, the train's loading. They'll go without you."

But she just keeps on singing: But there's one thing I know / these blues they sent to meet me / won't defeat me. . . .

And her voice is strong sure of itself, different from her body.

"Com'on," she says to me, "it's beautiful out here."

"We've gotta go." I say. I don't want to get wet.

144

"Cryin's not for me," she sings, "cause I'm never gonna stop the rain by complaining / because I'm free / nothing worrying me."

And then she stops and looks at me intently and it's like everybody I've ever known is looking at me all at once.

"What're you scared of?" she says.

And I think for a moment. "Nothing, I guess."

"Rigghhtt." And then she runs through the doorway past me. And I run after her, not to catch up. I'm worried about missing the train. And as I get on I realize I don't want to catch up to anybody. I just want to learn to be a little more brave.

Library of Congress Catalogue Card No. 74-76141
ISBN 0 88750 103 6 (hardcover)
ISBN 0 88750 104 4 (softcover)

Cover by Christopher Pratt courtesy National Gallery of Canada. Book design by Michael Macklem.

Printed in Canada by the Hunter Rose Company

PUBLISHED IN CANADA BY OBERON PRESS

DATE DUE

AU	